Vestigia

Vestigia

By

Francis X. Levy

Ad Majorem Dei Gloriam

An Autobiography

Llumina Press

© 2005 Francis X. Levy

All rights reserved. No part of this publication may be reproduced or transmitted in any form or by any means electronic or mechanical, including photocopy, recording, or any information storage and retrieval system, without permission in writing from both the copyright owner and the publisher.

Requests for permission to make copies of any part of this work should be mailed to Permissions Department, Llumina Press, PO Box 772246, Coral Springs, FL 33077-2246

ISBN: 1-59526-506-6 PB
       1-59526-512-0 HC

Printed in the United States of America by Llumina Press

Library of Congress Control Number: 2005934606

Contents

Acknowledgments	i
Foreword	iii
Preface	v
Very Early Years	1
As a Child	3
As a Youth	19
Wartime	39
Marriage	63
Another War	69
Joining Industry	79
Disguised Grace	91
Mary Naughten	97
Retirement	111
Wonderful Memories	117
My Mother	133
The Greatest Gift	137
Our Lady	139
Afterthoughts	141
Addendum	147
Lagniappe	149

To My Wife Mary

A dedicated Pro-Lifer for the Unborn
and their Vulnerable Mothers

Acknowledgments

My wife, Mary, provided major assistance in bringing this book to fruition. She is my constant editor and assistant and, in fact, the very reason I even attempted to write. Without her, there would be no book.

My sister Mary Levy Brown has kindly complied with my request and created three pieces of art expressly for this publication. In addition to these original drawings, she has been my principal aid in the assembly of our family tree. I am also grateful to the many members of our family who have provided the necessary tree details.

Patricia Treece, a gifted writer and model of Catholic virtue, has been a true source of encouragement; her books are forever an inspiration. Her Foreword, which follows, is deeply appreciated but undeserved.

Cover photo of the Holy Father with Francis and Mary Levy was taken at the Vatican on March 7, 1997. Copyright L'OSSERVATORE ROMANO 00120 CITTA DEL VATICANO SERVIZIO FOTOGRAFICO. Printed with permission.

Foreword

Francis X. Levy is one of those rare persons who truly will do anything for a friend. Totally given to God, he loves to help those who he believes are doing God's work. A Eucharistic minister, he and his wife, Mary (who has her own apostolate in the Right to Life Movement), bring the Eucharist to homebound ill or dying people. They also bring caring, love, and prayer and its power.

Francis Levy has written this book as an extension of that ministry so that all who read it may know the power of prayer. This is an autobiography, but it is truly not about Francis so much as about prayer. Francis is not a self-centered person. He has no desire to write his life so that people will applaud his achievements. What he wants to share with you, the reader, is that God is faithful, God is loving, God is kind: God is indeed the Good Shepherd. In anecdote after anecdote, Francis shows how even in the most difficult times, God has walked with him and with his loved ones.

In his earlier book on mystic Father Aloysius Ellacuria, CMF, *Our Guide*, Francis Levy showed the power of prayer through the life and actions of a holy priest who greatly influenced the Levy family.

I heartily recommend both books to you for the encouragement they give to belief in the reality, power, and love of a living God. Francis and his wife, Mary, have long been an inspiration to me, and I can attest personally, as I said at the opening of this little Foreword, that Francis and Mary are truly people who will do anything for a friend. I have benefited many times from their enormous generosity and their helpfulness, their kindness, and, above all, their example—not only of Christian marriage but of individuals given completely to the service of Christ. So I recommend these books to you, especially this little book before you, not only for what they contain but because they are written by a man who truly does his best to live every moment in the presence of God and to not only preach the Gospel but to reveal it through his life. May the Lord help you and me follow his example.

Patricia Treece

Preface

Everybody has a story to tell, because every life is important. Life is a gift from God, and that is what makes it important. Some lives are very eventful, whereas others seem to be rather routine. How long we live or how many accolades we amass are not the necessary criteria for success. How we respond to God's Grace and then influence others by our actions to turn their eyes toward our Creator should be our primary goal. Each person is to reflect in his own unique way the God-given attributes that make him who he is. I've spent my life attempting to discern these attributes.

I have often heard people say, "If only I had my life to live over again…" I think that is a good sign, because it indicates that one has learned something about life and from then on will surely act accordingly to move toward perfection. We tend to apply our own standards and make judgments based on conclusions that seem to us so obvious. Would that we all could judge as He alone is capable. I often pray that somewhere, somehow, some little thing that I may have done will glorify God and bring a soul within His grasp.

My life is no more important than any other, but it does have its share of special events. I relate some of those events in these pages as a means of information and as an impetus for others to learn from my mistakes and thereby make better use of their lives.

There is definitely one aspect of my life that is most noteworthy. It is the fact that I have been the recipient of many graces, none of which I deserved. And God has bountifully answered my prayers in dramatic ways. Clearly He indicates the mercy and love that He has for each of us, even for me. There are many instances in these pages that give dramatic proof of God's loving response to my requests. And oh, how thankful I am that He has chosen in so many cases to deny me those things that I was absolutely sure I wanted.

We all have our own style of prayer, and maybe it takes a lifetime to find out what is best for us. I prefer meditation to vocal prayer; I get too distracted in prolonged vocal prayer and find that I am constantly prodding myself into awareness. Of course, both types are fruitful and necessary, but we do have our preferences.

Many times Mary has asked me to write my journal. Many times I have turned a deaf ear to this request. But now, for whatever it is worth, I will try. I cannot adequately express my gratitude for her assistance in this endeavor.

I am the fifth of nine children born to Albert Allen Levy and Henrietta Catherine Schaeffer in New Orleans, Louisiana. We are: Maxine, Gertrude, Muriel, Albert, Francis, Mary, Joseph, Michael, and Louis. Because my father did not approve of nicknames for us, we were always called by our full names. Actually, there were twelve children—three died at birth. I came on June 10, 1925, and was given the name of Francis Xavier, after the great Jesuit Missionary. The name was appropriate at the time, because my father was studying law at Loyola University, a Jesuit institution.

Even though I am not a missionary like my namesake, it has been my lifelong ambition to travel. Thanks be to God, this desire has come to fruition. I have seen many countries and beautiful cities, but Rome is my favorite. It has fascinated me ever since I first visited there in 1979. Even though I would have to learn another language in order to live there, I would accept the challenge. In deference to the Latin of the early Romans, I call my journal *Vestigia*: "Footsteps."

Chapter One

Very Early Years

*H*enry Schaeffer, my maternal grandfather, walked along the path by the box step at the front of his house. He carried a lantern because it was dusk there on Liberty Street. It had to be 1927, because that was the last year that he lived and the earliest year that I could have remembered. I don't know what month it was—probably fall or winter, because I had turned two years of age the preceding June. My older brother, Albert, sat with me. This was the beginning of our friendship as close buddies, united in the cause of male superiority—a cause that was forever threatened by the existence of three older sisters.

As a baby, I was very irritable, and at times my mother had to put up with a lot of crying. Nothing she could do would quiet me. When I frequently suffered with stomach distress years later, I tended to relate this condition to the one in my babyhood. Ultimately I learned that I have difficulty digesting milk. Perhaps this was the underlying cause of my childhood distress.

Years elapsed until my next memories—probably 1929—when Marx Levy, my paternal grandfather, played patriotic music for us on a hard rubber, cylindrical recording. He was a devout Orthodox Jew who visited the sick at Charity Hospital on Sundays and brought toys to the children there. Curiously I would look into his armoire whenever I could, just to see what toys he was accumulating to bring to the hospital. At times he took care of us younger children when other members of the family had to go out, and we loved the candy—silver bells—that he gave us on frequent occasions. When he spoke, you knew he had authority. He could talk to me about anything and I would gobble it up. Grandpa lived with us, and my father called him "Papa." At the dinner table he had a routine that he practiced with my mother when he wanted a napkin: "Henrietta, you got an old dish towel or a mop or something?" Then, in another situation, whenever my mother raised her voice as she sometimes did in order to communicate afar, Grandpa would step out on the back gallery, face the direction of the street at the other end of the house and call out, "You can go home now, Couvertier," as though we had aroused the storekeeper one half block down the street. Marx was a railway mail clerk, and he had a .38 caliber pistol to carry on his job. This gun has long been a cherished possession of mine. He also had a large, silver-colored pocket watch, which I kept for many years as a memento before passing it on to one of my children.

One night in 1930, when my father was out of town on business, Marx died in bed in the hallway near my room, which itself was a small hallway. My sister Maxine helped my mother care for him during his last hours. As a child of about five, I heard the conversations as they went on during the night, and I knew that a grave situation existed.

Chapter Two

As a Child

Fortunately, there was a time when my mother had a black lady come in every day to help with the housework. Carrie Turner was as sweet a lady as you would want to meet. For $7 a week plus car fare, she would come and work all day. Carrie would bathe Albert and me in the tub in the bathroom on the back gallery. Whenever Carrie was sick and unable to come to our house to work, her cousin, Juliet Barnett Hunter, would come over. In her we were blessed again with a wonderfully sweet lady. I always felt sorry for Juliet because she had a large protruding lower lip which was caused by a stroke that she had had.

As youngsters, we became aware of the dreadful position that the Negroes held in our society, unofficially classified as second-class citizens. At home we were taught that all men are created equal in the eyes of God, and surely we were to treat all of God's creatures with love and respect. In the outside world, however, it was a different story. I remember black people being served at restaurants, waiting outside for food to be brought to them, since they were not allowed to go inside. At times I remember a black man asking me to go inside a restaurant for him to bring something out. More shameful than this was the situation with the restrooms. It was the general policy for public buildings such as train stations and bus stations to have four restrooms—two for blacks and two for whites. In those instances where there were only white restrooms, the blacks were just out of luck. On streetcars and buses, blacks had to sit in the back behind a movable sign that marked their section.

Even in church, although it was not marked as such, there was a section that was understood to be the "colored section." Frequently, I made it my business to sit in this area with the "colored people" so that they might know that we loved and respected them as being no different than we were.

There was a black man in the French Quarter who was called "Bae-Bae." He had a wonderful muscular build and seemed to be of a mild nature, but for some reason, he would run afoul of the law. Then one day, I heard that he had died in jail. I wonder how he died. Until this time, I had thought that the police could do no wrong.

The political situation in Louisiana has always been colorful but sometimes tumultuous. The Democratic Party has been firmly entrenched for ever so long. The local faction was called the Old Regulars. I had difficulty understanding why the two-party system didn't provide a viable means for correcting the corruption that existed. When politicians fled to Canada, the "hot oil" scandal became somewhat hilarious nationally.

In second grade we began receiving free pencils, paper, and books. I don't know what people did before that if they didn't have enough money to buy these supplies. This was the era of Huey Long. The "Kingfish," as he was called, established dictatorial power to advance his program of economic and social reform. He was elected governor in 1928 at the age of 35, but in only two more years he advanced to the U.S. Senate. Only after he had selected his replacement as governor of Louisiana did he resign that office, but even then he maintained complete control of state functions from Washington.

I found the programs of this regime very interesting, and surely I benefited from them. A paving program was started throughout the state in order to improve the woeful condition of our highways. The slogans we heard in those days were "A chicken in every pot" and "A car in every garage." An annual income of $5000 was the goal for all. "Every man a king" was the phrase of the time. Politically, Louisiana had arrived on the national scene. Our advocator, Huey Pierce Long, was grandiloquent and flamboyant. His popularity increased when he presented his Share the Wealth program, and it wasn't too long before he aspired to the presidency. But in September 1935, even though he had an entourage of bodyguards, he was shot in a corridor of the State Capitol in Baton Rouge. His assassin was the son of a political enemy. Soon, the "Extra" edition of the newspaper was on the streets as the newsboys shouted the headlines. This was my introduction into Louisiana politics. When I endeavor to explain Huey Long to anyone, I suggest that they read his autobiography and then read a biography. Then you get the picture. Years later, my decision to follow the advice of Horace Greeley and go west had three motives: Louisiana politics, Louisiana climate, and Louisiana economics. I knew that California wouldn't be Utopia, but I was sure it would be better.

Vestigia

Every group of kids has its bully. Ours was called "Blackie." Whenever he was around, all of the boys scattered for fear they would have to face the dreaded Blackie. All, that is, except one: Clifton St. Germain; he would stand up to anyone. Rarely did he have to prove this point, because in that kind of society you generally did it just once. I saw him demonstrate his boxing skills on some occasions—he was really good and the word got around. It soon became common knowledge that Clifton liked my sister Muriel, but that's as far as it ever got; she never heard it directly from him. However, whenever Blackie was near, Clifton made it his business to protect Albert and me. I think that was his way of communicating with Muriel. Clifton not only was a very likeable guy, but he proved to be an invaluable bodyguard.

My maternal grandmother lived with us for several years and was a great friend of mine. Before she finally came to stay with us, she had been moving around from time to time with her other relatives. She had been with Auntie (Agnes Hayden), my mother's older sister, and also with Aunt Mag (Maggie Bulliung), my grandmother's sister. Aunt Mag herself was living on Jefferson Davis Parkway with her daughter, Marguerite Davis, whose husband taught driving. Marguerite had a sister, Lillian, whose situation I was never fully aware of. Maybe Granny also stayed with her son, Herbert, at this time. We always called him "Uncle" to avoid confusing him with my father's brother, Arthur Herbert, whom we called "Uncle Herbert." One day we received word that Uncle had been found dead behind the wheel of his car. This was a loss for me—I liked him a lot. He and Aunt Vera had visited us often.

When Granny was in her sixties, she played ball with my brother Albert and me. Granny's maiden name was Ruth—I recall hearing somewhere that she was a relative of Babe Ruth. Granny loved to cook and bake. When she baked pies, she made a special one for me; I was flabbergasted. She was everything that a grandmother was supposed to be, and I always knew that she liked me. Very often I would see her sitting in her room in the darkness praying the Rosary. Sometimes, years later, Mother assigned me to take Granny around the corner to confession at St. Mary's Church on Saturday. She still recalled some German expressions from her youth, and in the forties when she was in a coma, she spoke in German. This coma lasted for several days, and I never expected her to survive, but she did. As she lay in bed, we kept a coal fire burning in the fireplace. That was where I learned to bank a fire for the night.

On occasion when Granny had a doctor's appointment and I was the one to take her, we traveled by streetcar. I would become infuriated when men did not get up to offer her a seat. When Auntie visited for the day, usually on Monday, she and Granny cooked red beans and rice. They liked to have Claret wine with their meal, so they sent me to Bourbon and Ursuline Streets, around the corner to Reboul's Winery, to buy a quart of bulk wine for about fifteen cents or a quarter. Then, at home, Granny and Auntie poured me a small glass of wine with some sugar in it. I don't know whose idea that was.

The Red Store, located in the French Market, was always an interesting place to visit with my father or grandfather. They even had an open barrel filled with sauerkraut. If the store couldn't hold your attention, there were the switch engines outside on the railroad tracks by the river. Another stop close by, across Decatur Street, was Horak's Bakery, with that captivating smell of freshly baked French bread. All you had to do was buy a couple of loaves at seven cents each and you could get a delicious cream doughnut for lagniappe. If you ever had a nickel, you could buy three of these doughnuts, the likes of which I never found again anywhere. The "Pretty Girl," as my grandfather called her, was our friendly smiling clerk. I'm not sure that she was especially pretty, but her pleasant personality exuded a special charm. I wonder if I ever knew her name.

On a few occasions, Mother accompanied Daddy on business trips. Maxine would be delegated to care for the younger children during their absence; she did a beautiful job each time. Of course there were minor spats that I had from time to time with my siblings, but I really loved each one of them, and they were all so good to me.

One time when Daddy and Mother were on a trip, Albert and I chased each other from room to room, and on each cycle through our bedroom we jumped up and ran across our bed. As I became fatigued, I didn't jump quite high enough to clear the angle iron at the foot of the bed, and I rapped my little toe. That toe already had a congenital deformity, and I compounded the problem. I'm sure I broke the toe, and it has never returned to its "normal" deformed condition. I didn't report this incident to Maxine, because I wasn't supposed to be running like this—I knew I was wrong.

There was a bank on Decatur Street that advertised an interest rate of 2.5% on savings. That didn't sound appealing to me because it was so low. I never had any money anyway, though, so it made no difference. This bank was close to the Progress Grocery and the Central Grocery, both of which carried a wide variety of exciting foods such as "brown paper" (imported dried apricot rolled into sheets). Brown paper was always a delicacy whenever one of my friends brought some to school. We also liked pumpkin seeds, but we rarely had money for snacks. Those were the days in grammar school when we seldom had a ball to play with so we substituted a cone from the nearby magnolia tree. Touch football was our favorite pastime during recess.

The ladies who sold fruit and vegetables in the open stands of the French Market got to know me, because I made frequent trips there in the mornings before school. Each way was about three or four blocks, and it seemed like a long way. My mother would say, "Francis, get a soup brisket and a soup bone in the meat market, and go to the vegetable stand and get a soup bunch—and ask for lagniappe" (which in most cases was parsley; I never remember having to buy parsley). Sometimes I had to make a special trip to the ice house on Decatur Street to get a block of ice for our icebox. After they wrapped it in newspaper, I would put it on my shoulder for the two-and-a-half-block journey home. That wasn't too far to go, but I used to hurry so that the least amount of water dripped on me. In later years, the circular icebox on the back gallery gave way to a huge Servel Electrolux refrigerator. I think it cost over $400, and it was run by natural gas. We didn't have that unit very long; it had some kind of a problem. I don't know what resolution there was, but soon we got an electric refrigerator. Either way, I was delighted not to have to carry ice anymore. Daddy used to make special desserts with this refrigerator, especially frozen cream cheese. Other treats that he prepared routinely in the kitchen were Boston brown bread, peanut brittle, and crystallized watermelon rind.

Often I would have the chore of going to Madonia's Grocery around the corner, on the "lake side" of Bourbon Street. Sometimes I used my skating truck (a homemade scooter of wood with old roller skates on the bottom), but most of the time I walked. On one occasion when I was walking, I was in the middle of crossing Bourbon Street when I looked up and was absolutely stunned to see the grill of a large truck right before my face—he had stopped in the nick of time! I even remember that this truck had hard rubber tires instead of the modern pneumatic type.

I liked to read the funny papers and had my particular preferences. One of these was a character named Boob McNutt. Well, one day,

Mother was making some eggnog, and she sent me to Madonia's for some nutmeg. When I got to the store, I had difficulty remembering the name of the ingredient that I was supposed to get. Then I decided that it was "mac-nut." Of course, Mrs. Madonia had no idea what I was looking for, and it was too expensive to make a five-cent phone call to inquire. So I went home and asked Mother for the right name of the ingredient—I had been close, but not close enough to be understood.

Our usual way of shopping for groceries was by phone. Mother phoned her order to Mrs. Madonia, and shortly thereafter, Emile, the black errand man, made the delivery. It was a momentous event when Emile arrived, because our dog, Lady, would signal his arrival even before the doorbell rang. Lady would tear down the twenty-four curving steps of the stairway and continue full speed down the hallway to the "gate." (We called the wooden door a gate.) It was either my job or the job of someone else who was close at hand to call Lady back upstairs and "lock her up" in Grandma's kitchen. When it was safe for Emile to proceed, we would go back downstairs, let him come in, and have him bring the groceries up to the "hall," a sort of living room. Then Mother checked the order, item by item, before paying Emile. Money was hard to come by, and certainly Mother knew it. She was sure that she got everything she paid for and paid for everything she got.

Sometimes, a horse-drawn wagon would stop by our house with produce for sale. The vendor would pull up directly in front of the house so that Mother could look straight down from the front gallery onto his wagon. Whatever she decided to buy would first have to be inspected by her, and then one of us children would go downstairs to buy it. In the case of watermelons, the vendor would "plug" the melon for inspection. If the section that he cut out wasn't "red to the rind," Mother didn't want it.

We all loved molasses. We just poured it onto a dish and sopped it up with French bread; sometimes we added cheddar cheese to augment the bread. What a delicious treat that was! I don't think we ever had maple syrup in the house; it was always molasses. Later I learned that I didn't care for maple syrup unless it was real maple. An easy lunch sometimes was bananas and bread or maybe bread, "butter," and sugar.

I don't remember when we ever had real butter on the table—we always had oleomargarine. I believe that Nucoa was one of the brands that came already colored, but some types were absolutely white. There was a small packet of dye that came in the box, and it was often my job to squeeze this little button of juice into the oleo and mix it until the batch looked like butter. As a kid, I didn't know why we went to this trouble just for visual appeal; it didn't add to the taste one bit.

In the evening, the milkman (M. Wicker Dairy) would leave our milk by the front gate. We would get 2 quarts or 2 quarts and 1 pint of raw milk. As a rule, I never liked milk, but I enjoyed cream cheese—even when we made it ourselves by allowing a bottle of milk to sit on the dining room window sill for a few days. I remember these particular events and also recall my delight on being able to spoon out the remnants of condensed milk from a recently emptied can. We used this milk in our coffee. When I did this, it wasn't unusual for the dog to be close at hand, anxious to join in the feast. One time, Albert and I used one spoon to alternate between the dog's mouth and ours. In due time, our festival was spotted and immediately corrected. Lady was spitz and collie; she was a wonderful dog.

What a great treat it was on the rare occasions that my father was able to take us to the Morning Call or the Café du Monde coffee stand for that delicious coffee and doughnuts—it was twenty-five cents or less for the coffee and the three doughnuts. Another desirable treat was the stop that we sometimes made on Dumaine and Royal Streets at Joe Napolitano's market for a Coke or 7-up after Mass on Sunday mornings. When you consider that we had been fasting from all food and drink from midnight the night before and now it was about 10:15 A.M. after the nine o'clock Mass on a hot, summer, southern day, you get the feel for the savor.

We never had chicken or turkey, because my father didn't like either. As a young man, it had been his job around home to kill the chickens, and he just had had enough of that. But we had a lot of pork that was absolutely delicious. Oysters, too, were plentiful and excellent.

On more than one occasion my father took me on his business trips either to Shreveport or Jackson. Apparently, since I was too young for school and also could travel free, it provided a means of babysitting. I remember how I learned all about the Pullman train cars and the collapsible bunks that the porter made up at night. I complained once to my father while in the diner because they had given me a multiplicity of tableware, whereas all I really needed was one fork. He enjoyed my comment so much that he often told that story. During the day, at the office where my father was working, he sometimes sat me by the window with a pencil and a pad of paper with the instructions to observe the switch engines outside and jot down the numbers of the engines. He prized my diligence and would always give me a new pad of paper the next day, even though I hadn't used up the whole pad. As I recall, he took the old pad to show off my work. We used to joke about my being asked by the conductor to state my age because I would say, "I'm five on the train, but I'm six at home."

When I was about five, I was tongue-tied. I used to say, "Twain twack." Daddy had a special technique that he used on me. He would tell me to say, "Ta-rain-ter-rack." So, dutifully, I would repeat, "Ta-rain-ter-rack." Feeling a sense of accomplishment, he would then tell me to say, "Train track." Immediately, I would respond with, "Twain twack."

Whenever I had a special project in school, Daddy was ready to help me even to the point of doing most of the work himself, as was the case when we made a cardboard airplane. I was crestfallen the next day when the big boys at school took it away from me and threw it around until they broke it.

When Daddy came home from work, he used to lie down in bed to read the paper. I'd wait for him to come home and listen for his whistle when he arrived at the front gate. No sooner was he settled comfortably, when I'd ask him, "Daddy, you want to play bears?" So that he could continue reading the paper, he would trap me with his arm or leg until I could break free, and then another limb would plop over me and the struggle would start anew.

I liked to play with toy automobiles, which I had been given from time to time. My favorite was a car with electric headlights. I enjoyed bringing it into a dark room or under a bed where the headlights were prominent. My big worry, of course, was that the batteries would burn out if I left the lights on too long. I realized that there wasn't any money for new batteries, so I had better be frugal.

Our parents' bedroom really was our living room. It was there that we did our homework and listened to the radio. One day while Daddy was reading the newspaper by the "reading light" (the lamp with the 100-watt bulb), I was by his feet playing on the floor with rolled-up silver balls made from the foil of Hershey candy kisses. I was making "bombing runs" right over the electrical plug of the reading light. As the tines of the plug did not fit snugly into the receptacle, the gap between these tines provided a "precision drop" challenge for my metallic, round bomb. Miss after miss after miss was at last followed by a direct hit, but lo, what happened then, just when I was successful—the light went out! Daddy bolted up to assess the situation and restore the power. He was puzzled; he didn't have a clue as to the cause of the power failure. When he darted downstairs to the front of the house to the fuse box, as usual I was right behind him. He used to explain to me how fortunate we were in that we had not only one, but two electrical circuits—one for upstairs and one for downstairs. When he had wired the house, he'd provided for this luxury. He admonished me never to put a penny behind the fuse as some people were prone to do in order to restore a burned fuse. Daddy knew that when there was a power failure, you must determine the cause and correct it before attempting to turn the power on again. But he was stymied this time. He didn't know what had caused the problem; therefore, he could not apply corrective action. His only alternative was to turn the power on again and hope that it would stay on. That he did, and successful he was. Then, with power restored, I went back to my "bombing runs." This time I explained to Daddy how strange it was that the light had gone out just as I had hit my target. Of course, this revelation turned a light on in his mind, and he solved the problem immediately—no more "bombing runs"!

There were three traumatic events in my early life. Actually, it was the same event repeated three times, occurring each time one of my sisters left to become a nun. In those days, such departure was considered, and truly meant to be, a separation from the family—to such a degree that they would never return home again even for a visit. It was possible that they would never even be seen by the family again. Even a death in the family would not be cause for an exception to this rule. With proper intervals for their differences in age, Maxine, Gertrude, and Muriel left home in this fashion. For me, it was as though each in her turn had died. Truly, I was crushed each time. If I ever hurt them, I was really sorry.

There wasn't anything Daddy couldn't do. Until this day, he remains the most talented person that I've ever met. He wasn't a genius in anything, but he was excellent in *everything*! He was a carpenter, an electrician, a musician, a cook, a weaver capable of building his own looms and weaving a blanket and rugs. Of course, he always had his helper by his side, because whether I liked it or not, my mother's instructions were to stay with Daddy. Among his accomplishments was the building of a short-wave radio. He listened to the coded stock broadcasts on the radio at night in order to learn Morse code. The guitar that he built was later passed on to a grandchild. He had numerous projects in his workshop and was very disappointed when a local school didn't welcome his homemade "Tesla coil"—a high-voltage device that can be used in a physics lab. The more I think about my father's talents, the more I remember. He practiced "Church Law" in Latin before the Matrimonial Court of the Archdiocese and also preached on street corners for the Catholic Evidence Guild. In his senior years, he taught French at St. Joseph's school. By this time, he had already taught himself calculus and German. His quest for knowledge extended into his seventies, when he enrolled in Louisiana State University in New Orleans for further study of history. His pursuit of knowledge was insatiable.

For most of my years in grammar school, my sister Gertrude was my proctor with the instruction to "hear" my lessons for the next day. Before this assignment was made, however, my father used to do the job himself. Once, after work, as he rested in bed, he asked me to read my lesson to him. I did a good job, but I surely startled him when I hit one word, "Gustava" (the name of the girl in the story). I said, "Gus-*stava*." He dropped the newspaper and said, "What?" So, I repeated, "Gus-*stava*." "Let me see that book," he said. "That's '*Gus*-tava,'" he said. In later years I realized that he fully understood that my flaw in pronunciation was due to the accent exhibited by our teachers, the Teresian Sisters, who were a Spanish-speaking order from Mexico.

For the rest of my life I truly thanked God for the love, devotion, and ability that these Sisters displayed—Mother Carmen in first grade, Mother Maria Mendez in second grade, Mother Maria in fourth grade (I skipped third grade), Mother Trinidad in fifth grade, Mother Mary Louise in sixth grade, and Mother Maria Mejia in seventh grade (we had no eighth grade). All this time, Mother Mary Agnes was the Principal. Mother Neavis taught kindergarten, while Mother Annunciata taught the second-grade girls.

During the winter it was often a cold and damp journey that we made, walking the five blocks to school. My poor, busy mother couldn't make many appealing lunches for us. I remember potted ham, dry cheese, and jam sandwiches, and I think we also had sardines. That was about it; there were no delicacies.

Vestigia

It was the policy of the Teresian Sisters to tell us to pray to Henri de Osso, their founder, whenever there was a need for special prayers. With this entreaty, they would place a third-class relic in our hands. Many years later, in 1979, while Mary and I were in Rome, we became aware of a ceremony that was soon to take place at St. Peter's; we had no idea what it was all about. As we walked past the many motor coaches, I caught sight of a small sign: "Henri de Osso." I kept on walking. Then, suddenly, it dawned on me who he was. So we inquired whenever we were able to make ourselves understood, trying to learn something of the forthcoming ceremony. At last we found out that Henri de Osso was going to be beatified! Wow! What a wonderful opportunity to witness this glorious event—if we could get in. It didn't take long to discover that you must have a ticket, and there were no more tickets available. Undaunted, we pursued our inquiry until we met a Teresian Sister who generously procured two passes for us to attend the next day's celebration. I believe that the nuns themselves sacrificed for us. We were then greatly privileged to sit in the third row and witness the beatification of this holy man in St. Peter's Basilica. God blessed our family's many years of prayer on behalf of Henri de Osso with the gift of attendance at this momentous event.

As my thoughts return to those early days on Royal Street, I remember that I was interested in printing. One day I heard that you could get a printing set at a reasonable price, and, therefore, I wanted one. Even though it was a very basic hand set wherein you had to hold each letter and then ink it before making an impression, I liked it. I became irate one day when I saw that my little brothers, Joe and Mike, had gotten into my precious printing set. Of course, at their age, if I had had the chance, I would have done the same thing.

The radio was a great means of entertainment in the days before television. Each night we had an opportunity to hear all sorts of programs that were decent, interesting, and marvelously presented. There was such class to these shows that I would rather have most of them available now in place of the present variety of television fare. We had the *Lux Radio Theater, Kraft Music Hall, Amos and Andy, The Jack Benny Show, Burns and Allen, Fibber McGee and Molly, Gangbusters, Gunsmoke, Your Hit Parade, Studio One, One Man's Family, The FBI in Peace and War, Playhouse 90,* and others. The element of realism that was achieved left nothing to be desired.

In the hall that served as our parlor, we had our one radio, an Atwater Kent, which was impressive with its many available frequency bands. By reaching into the rear of the cabinet of this radio, we could throw a "knife switch" that hooked up the remote large, circular speaker in my parents' bedroom. Two locations were then available for our listening pleasure.

I remember the time I failed to heed my father's instructions for switching the speaker control. We were supposed to turn the power off before reaching into the back of the radio. Somehow I wasn't synchronized, and my left hand, which was to turn the power off, lagged behind while the right hand was right on schedule. Wham! I really got a shock. It was the kind you remember for a long time—a rather invaluable experience.

There was a World's Fair in 1933 and 1934, which my parents attended in Chicago; Maxine and Gertrude went to the Fair, also. This was about the same time we got the wonderful Atwater Kent radio; I believe my father bought it at the Fair.

All of us children played downstairs in our yard, because we had few parks and the streets of the French Quarter in which we lived were particularly dangerous. Essentially, we had either the schoolyard or our own backyard for our recreational activities. Albert and I always played together, and occasionally Muriel would join us. But we didn't think that she ought to have a turn at bat—after all, she was a girl. When we were rather young, it was a fearsome thing for someone to walk onto the back gallery when Albert and I were batting the ball in the yard. The ball would go flying up onto the gallery, and if that wasn't dangerous enough, sometimes it would hit the ceiling and knock down a hail of plaster.

One time I was pushing Louis around on his tricycle. While I had one foot on the rear axle, I propelled us both with the other foot and used both of my hands for steering. Around and around the yard we went. Each time we got to the French doors at the end of the yard, I turned the bike around so that we could continue our trip. Finally, when I wanted to quit, I decided that Louis would know what I was doing when I hopped off—and left the coasting tricycle for him to steer around the turn at the French doors. Poor Lou didn't know what was going on, and he (about four years old) went crashing through the glass panes of these French doors. He bore the marks of the horrible gash that he received and his numerous stitch marks for the rest of his life.

Vestigia

Like every house in the French Quarter where we lived, we had roaches, mosquitoes, bedbugs, and rats. Daddy set many rat traps. I know, because I was always with him. We sat side by side in the hall upstairs, him with his .22 caliber rifle on his lap. From this location, he could lean out of the window, overlooking the yard, and shoot the rats. Or he could face the attic stairway and catch them in transit. Those were exciting days! After these exploits, I learned how to clean a gun, because Daddy always took proper care of his rifle. Often he used this same rifle for target practice on the levee. One of his friends, Mr. Fassy, went with us on these excursions. Daddy also had a Colt .45 pistol, but I don't remember ever seeing him fire it.

I liked the levee wherever we encountered it. New Orleans depends on many levees for protection from the Mississippi; therefore, they became familiar to me. While on a hike one day with the altar boys and Father Moore, we had no drinking water. The boys solved that problem by going down to the bank of the river and scooping up some nice-looking, bubbly water at the crest of a wave. The next day all of us were sick.

As in most households, Daddy took care of business and Mother ran the house. He called her "Girl" and she called him "Boy." Since I knew the delineation of authority, I never appealed over my mother's head—but on occasion, I did argue. Every Saturday, Albert and I had to sweep the yard. It was not necessary to say that we didn't like it, as all one had to do was look for himself; we didn't show any exuberance.

I felt sorry for Daddy whenever we broke a window of the French doors while we were playing ball in the yard; that meant another repair job for him. In fact, sometimes we shattered a door with our hard throws; it didn't always require a batted ball to accomplish this. Mother constantly came to our defense by telling Daddy, "Boy, that's the only place they can play." Daddy responded by building metal screens in front of all the glass panes. That was not sufficient protection, however, because eventually we depressed these screens so much that they in turn hit the glass and broke it.

Another Saturday event in our house was the Metropolitan Opera broadcast on the radio. We were obliged to sit and listen to this, even though we had no use whatsoever for it. I remember the time that all of us children were elated because the regular broadcast was cancelled one Saturday. Our joy was short lived when we were presented with the alternate plan of my father. We had to gather around the wind-up phonograph and play a recording of the light opera *HMS Pinafore*, or some such Gilbert and Sullivan composition, and follow it line by line with the score in front of us. I thought that this was worse than the usual presentation of the operas.

I tended to view our family in groups. Maxine and Gertrude, being the eldest, comprised the first group. Since their ages were about six to eight years senior to me, they were always in a different category. For instance, when they were dating the Randon boys, Fulcron and Paul, Albert and I used to peek through the curtains out into the hall. The Randons were a well-respected family who had their home and dry cleaning establishment on Dauphine Street near our school.

Muriel, Albert, and I formed the second group. It seems that we had all the work to do. Of course, we were never overworked, but I had such a disdain for work at that time that it seemed to me to be ubiquitous.

The final group was Mary, Joe, Mike, and Louis. Sometimes they seemed like a different family because they were so young; their activities were apart from ours. Fortunately, in later years, I feel that I did become quite close to each one individually, and I cherish those friendships.

Of course, there had to be overlapping activities in these groups, such as the dancing classes. The three oldest girls attended a dancing school where they learned toe dancing. I used to ask Mother why they had to stand on their toes.

A typical early morning school-day routine in our house was the ironing of middy blouses and skirts by my mother and my sisters. This procedure was done in the kitchen in order to make use of the burners on the stove to heat the flatiron. All of this activity in the kitchen created a very busy environment at breakfast time with so many to feed. Mother often cooked oatmeal for us before we left for school, and if she became too involved in the ironing or in the fixing of breakfast for Daddy, or in getting us up for school, or in the selection of clothes for us to wear, or in any of the many other things necessary to run a house, then the outcome would be burned oatmeal. And that doesn't taste good at all! My poor Mother had such busy days that they sometimes resulted in burned beans for supper. When these things happened, I felt sorry for myself because I had to eat the food. In fact, I never thought that my mother was a very good cook. What an enlightenment I had in later years. When everyone grew up and she was unencumbered, it was an absolute delight to eat in her kitchen. Her gravies, her spaghetti and meat balls, her stuffed peppers, her bread pudding, her pork roasts, her yams, her shrimp stew—everything was tops!

Chapter Three

As a Youth

Albert and I played football frequently in the yard, most of the time without a real football. In fact, a good football was a cherished treasure; I don't remember ever owning one that was of any quality. One day we had a football game in our yard with Pete Finney, one of the younger altar boys. The game became too frisky for Pete; he got knocked down and didn't move. Albert and I were scared to death because we knew that Pete had had a terrible accident when he was two years old—he had fallen off a ladder and split his head open. The long scar that he had from that accident was often a discussion piece. We just knew now that we must have hit Pete on this tender area and now he was going to die. Hurriedly, we picked him up and raced up the steps to place him in my mother's bed—that was where you went whenever you were sick; Pete belonged there. Fortunately, he regained consciousness after a few minutes and fully recovered; in fact, he has been the Sports Editor for the New Orleans newspaper for many years.

I liked to play baseball even though I didn't have the bodily frame to do well in that sport. Most of the time, we played softball at the school on Saturday or at night when we could get into the schoolyard. Although the gate was locked at night, we simply climbed over the fence and turned the lights on. The Sisters in the convent right above could surely hear us, but they were kind enough to accept our noise, knowing that they were keeping us off the street.

I did manage to get on one of the teams at Jesuit High School, and it was then that I really had a good glove. I paid $5 for it using the money that I had saved. During these times, my godfather, Oliver Heyden, used to give me a dollar for all notable occasions. Until this time, I had only those cheap baseball gloves with a loose inner lining that would come out of the glove. It was very frustrating.

While Muriel, Albert, and I were in grammar school, Muriel came down with scarlet fever. We knew that this was a bad thing, but we also saw the good side—the house was quarantined, which obviously kept us home from school. Then when Mike got scarlet fever and, later, diphtheria, we again enjoyed quarantine. This time, however, I was somewhat older and felt the gravity of the situation. This was the first occasion I can remember of witnessing the power of prayer—Mike pulled through this crisis.

I think that I made my First Communion on May 6, 1932, when I was in second grade. It was the month of the Blessed Mother, and that was the regular schedule at the St. Louis Cathedral School. First Communion was an extremely solemn event. We preceded it with a three-day retreat, which I enjoyed. The days were spent in prayer and meditation, and Mother gave me money to buy lunch in the "candy store," as we called it. There was no greater day prior to my First Communion, and there has been none since. Frequently at Communion time I recall that momentous experience and I live it all over again. I know that I cannot truly get the message across when I talk to new communicants and tell them that this day is the greatest day of their lives. I beg for prayers from them on this occasion, for I know of no moment that is more opportune.

Again at Confirmation time we had a three-day retreat, and some of the boys tried to frighten us about the ceremony because Archbishop Rummel was going to slap each of us on the cheek in the symbolic gesture of preparation for suffering for our faith. It, too, was a most holy and auspicious occasion. Now we were Spiritual Soldiers. I was twelve, I believe, and one of the happiest situations then was to visit people as a Solemn Communicant and receive money. I never collected much, though.

It was the rule in our house that you didn't speak at the dinner table unless you were spoken to or unless you wanted to address our parents. I never actually heard the rule verbalized, but believe me, I understood it. In that way, even though we had a full dinner table (often with ten of us at one time), it was a quiet setting.

It was also a rule that everybody had to play music. My plight at first was to be the drummer in the grammar school band, which Daddy directed. I know that I was a first-class challenge to Daddy when I repeatedly beat the drums out of tempo. I also developed my own problem, the bass drum sliding across the floor every time I hit my foot pedal. I couldn't understand this action, because we had two sharp spikes attached to the rim of the drum, and they were pointed into the wooden floor. But slide it did—what a nuisance. After some time I was promoted to the soprano saxophone; that was a lot better. But I still didn't like to play music, and when your father is directing the band, that makes it even more difficult. Muriel and Albert shared this situation with me, and I think they enjoyed it as much as I did. I remember three of the selections that we played: "Happy Days," "Pilgrim's Chorus" from *Tannhaüser*, and "Barcarolle" from *The Tales of Hoffman*. Additionally, we had our own family band at home. Whenever company arrived, mostly relatives, we were summoned by Daddy to get our instruments and play for them. Daddy accompanied us on the piano. I have no idea what they ever thought of our music. While we were playing, I thought it was not so good.

Like all kids, I loved sports, and I thought I was a good sprinter. I was skinny and fast. When we had the Catholic School Athletic League (CSAL) track meet, a city-wide event, I participated in the dash and the broad jump while I was in sixth grade. Nobody will ever remember that, because I achieved very little. The next year, however, I did much better, coming in second in my heat in the dash as I tripped and fell across the finish line. I was thus selected for the next qualifying heat, where I placed second again. (There were so many boys in this track meet that we needed numerous heats.) Then it came time for the fifty-yard dash final race to see who would win the medals. Shortly after the race began, I sensed how crowded we were. There was insufficient space across the track to accommodate all of us, and it was soon too late in such a short race for me to move past anybody, as we were elbow to elbow. That's a good excuse, anyway, and I felt pretty good seeing my name appear twice in the newspaper the next day for doing so well in the qualifying heats.

Our home on Royal Street was beset by noise from the trolleys outside. Right in front of the house we had the Gentilly streetcar and the Desire, as well. Then at the corner of Ursuline there was the City Park car. Even though Royal was a narrow, one-way street, we still had automobile parking on both sides of it. It was not infrequent to have the motorman of the streetcar stop and clang his bell at the protruding autos. Then, too, it was sometimes necessary for the conductor to join with the motorman to physically rock the offending car off the tracks. It was even worse in the years preceding asphalt paving. Then the street was paved with wooden blocks, which frequently became dislodged and scattered haphazardly when victimized by the rains.

When I was a teenager and had been out at night, sometimes I tried to disguise my arrival home by standing on the banquette at the front door of our house and waiting until a streetcar was coming with its attendant noise. Then I would place my key in the lock, dash up the hallway and the twenty-four steps, and then race the distance down the hallway to my bed. Just when I thought I had gotten into bed undetected, it wasn't unusual for Mother to hear me in the next room and call out, "Is that you, son?"

Another exhilarating venture with my father was going to the Pearl Restaurant on St. Charles Avenue and Canal Street, where we stood at the oyster bar and ate a dozen raw oysters just as they were taken out of the shell. The men who did the shucking were particularly skilled, and I enjoyed just watching them. It was a problem for me anytime I went to an oyster house to decide whether I wanted raw or fried oysters. After this experience, I became convinced in later years that there were no better oysters in the world than those found in the Gulf of Mexico.

Whenever there was a fire in the French Quarter, it was categorized immediately as a General Alarm (a major fire that called for extra engines) because of the precarious and historic nature of the edifices. It was automatically understood that at the first sound of the fire engines, my father would dash out of the house and head for the scene of the fire, followed by any of the children who were interested. I always was right behind him, and Albert was there, as well.

At our house, an eclipse was a major event—be it total or partial, solar or lunar, we would never miss it. Daddy would prepare smoked glass for each of us to adequately protect our eyes. For this purpose, he always had old five-by-seven glass photographic plates available. After scraping the image off of the glass, the smoke from the flame of a candle provided the necessary smudge.

When I was about six years old, I joined the St. Louis Cathedral Altar Boys under the direction of Father Moore, O.M.I., an Irishman. He used to come to our house sometimes and sing while Daddy played the piano. During the week, the daily Masses were at 6:00, 6:30, and 7:00. When we were assigned to serve one of these Masses, it would be for the entire week, and that wasn't easy. The most difficult aspect was the fasting from midnight for Communion. Additionally, there was the terrible heat and humidity that we bore in the summer months because there was no air conditioning in the church. Most of the time there was no fan, and inside that cassock and surplice it was stifling. Day after day,

Vestigia

Creole staircase in the French Quarter

during the long Mass, I would feel faint and get a cold sweat, and yet never did I dare leave the altar. I placed that stringent requirement on myself because I was embarrassed. Whenever I had some kind of legitimate excuse to move around on the altar, I took advantage of the opportunity because it alleviated my distress.

There were frequent funerals in our parish, and Albert and I had to serve a lot of them because we were readily available. Mother saw to that. If there was to be a funeral, we hoped that it would be a military one so that we would have a long ride to the cemetery and see a stirring ceremony. Such a ceremony took place during a funeral Mass one day. How well I remember when the bugler blew "Taps" right in the front doorway of the Cathedral at the time of the Consecration. To make it even more impressive, that salute was followed immediately by a distant rendition of "Taps" from across the way in the Jackson Square. Of course, "Taps" was again blown at the gravesite, and then from afar it was echoed again. The final salute by the three rifle volleys at the gravesite provided an awesome conclusion. After a visit to the mortuary or after a funeral, Albert and I were taught by Daddy to wash our hands and face. I believe that this practice must have been Jewish in origin; I never actually checked it out.

Because of my involvement in the St. Louis Cathedral altar boys, I frequently went on picnics, trips to the ice cream parlor, and other outings. Father Edward B. Postert, O.M.I., was absolutely a great priest and a great friend of the boys. God provided him as a special gift, because he was exactly the kind of leader that we needed.

There was no finer athlete than my brother Albert, who was fast and agile. He played football and softball with abandon. He was a homerun hitter, a sprinter, and a distance runner. He never gave up on anything. When playing basketball he could usually last only for about a quarter or so before he fouled out. I felt that he was really playing football on the basketball court.

Albert was a constant companion of mine. On one occasion when we were swimming at Pontchartrain Beach, I had over-estimated my ability when swimming off the pier. When I got tired, I tried to touch bottom for a rest, but there was no bottom. Immediately, Albert noticed my plight and, from behind, gave me the necessary push back to the pier.

As I grew older, I was assigned to join the cleanup crew of Albert and Muriel in the kitchen. I hated it, and they didn't like it, either. Usually, Muriel washed the dishes, Albert dried them, and I swept the floor. The constant battle and of major importance then was to determine whose responsibility it was to clear off the table! According to our procedure, I couldn't sweep the floor until the table was wiped off because whoever wiped off the table brushed the crumbs onto the floor.

Because Daddy was a member of the Knights of Columbus, I became acquainted with the title of "Grand Knight." Albert and I used this knowledge to formulate a special title. We dubbed Muriel the "Grand Knight." Jokingly we held an election for this honor, but she knew that the reason she was always the winner was the fact that we cheated in her favor. Muriel was a good sport.

The St. Louis Cathedral School was five blocks from home, and it was an uncomfortable journey on the damp, cold days of winter when the temperature dipped into the low thirties and sometimes into the twenties. On our way home from school, Albert and I went down Bourbon Street instead of Royal, in order to avoid passing the McDonough 15 School, where we felt that we would get "beat up." In any event, we were both very fast, and that was our sure means of escape. We never did have an encounter in that neighborhood, and therefore I wonder if the fear was merely in our heads.

Most of my clothes were hand-me-downs that came to me from my cousins Allison and Herbert, but only after Albert, too, had had the use of them, if appropriate. It was thus that I remember once having two pairs of pants for school—one pair of short pants and one pair of knickers. When given the opportunity, I always put on the knickers, because I abhorred short pants. If, however, it was time for my pants to be washed, mother made me wear the red short pants. To avoid this, I'd try to rush out of the house before she could catch me.

It seems to have been in 1937 that a major renovation of the French Market took place. To celebrate the occasion, the city staged a dedication ceremony, which was hosted by Boy Scout Troop 95 of the St. Louis Cathedral. I remember the day when we gathered for the flag-raising. I think we got free coffee and doughnuts.

During my time in the Scouts, I remember three different scoutmasters—my father, Father Postert, and Mr. Leon Edmonds. This latter man was a stickler for drill maneuvers. I think he used to be a corporal or sergeant in the army, and every week we had what we considered to be military drills. He didn't like us to play the conventional sports that we favored, like softball or football. We were forced to play "scout games" like "steal the bacon." We liked Father Postert better, because he was more lenient.

There was a very fine Boy Scout camp outside of Slidell on the other side of Lake Pontchartrain. We couldn't afford to go there often, but when we could, it was great. The wooden cabins slept eight and had Indian names such as Chula, Chukfi, Shukata, Fala, Afhoma, Tiak Boko, and several others. The free-flowing well-water always smelled like rotten eggs, and it drained into Bayou Liberty.

In our Scout troop sometimes there were boxing matches as part of our games. My turn to fight one day pitted me against a durable slugger. I felt like I was no match for him, but since it was set up that way, I had to follow through with the schedule and be prepared to take my licks. Bobby Canedo was just about my age, but he was built solidly and possessed a wild haymaker of a punch. The trick to beating him was to be able to detect this whopping punch in its preparation stages and take due precaution. We punched and sparred and slugged—I guess we were quite even—and then, to my surprise, I found myself talking to one of my buddies as we sat side by side on a bench. Soon I came to realize that I had become a victim of one of Bobby's haymakers and had been knocked senseless; I was sitting on the bench because the fight was over. There was good news, however: I was told that the fight had to be stopped because I had inflicted a bloody nose on my opponent. I guess you'd say I won that one when I was out of my mind.

Also in 1937, when I was in seventh grade and it was time for me to graduate, Mother took me to Rubenstein's store on Camp and Canal to get a white suit. She wanted to get short pants for me, whereas everybody else in my class was buying long pants. She used to say that I looked like a dwarf in long pants. As hard as I tried to convince her that I needed long pants, I struck out. My savior, however, and the one to whom I'll forever be grateful, was the salesman at the store. He sided with my position emphatically and, thankfully for me, he made my mother concede.

One time I went to Loyola Stadium to see Loyola's football team play Mississippi State. During this era, the Wrigley Gum people had a promotion campaign going wherein they would offer to pay a crisp, new one-dollar bill to anyone whom they encountered that had some Wrigley's gum. Well aware of this great opportunity, I always carried such an item with me. Of course, I was too young to realize the odds that were stacked against me in this promotion. Nevertheless, while attending this game, during the halftime, as my buddies went to the snack stand and I sat alone, a man approached me (I was about 12 then) and asked if I had a pack of gum. "Oh yes," I replied, and immediately dug down in my pocket to produce it. Deeper and deeper I went until I reached an empty bottom. Now I realized that just before I had left home, my mother had instructed me to change pants for the game. Thus, no gum. Instead, this representative of Wrigley gave me a printed handout that served as a reminder of my ill luck. I thought I was the unluckiest guy in the world.

When I was about the same age, I remember I walked up Royal Street and had gotten to Toulouse, where I was obliged to wait for the traffic to clear. An open-top sedan stopped right before me as the driver waited for the Royal Street traffic to open up. In this sedan were about four men. One of the men in the back seat caught my attention because he looked awfully familiar. As the car lay stopped and I stood motionless, I looked and looked. When I arrived home a couple of hours later and read the newspaper, I learned that my recognition had been correct—it really was Franklin Roosevelt who was in New Orleans that day. This incident was also on my mind several years later when I saw President Eisenhower by the Jackson Square when he visited the city for a particular celebration. It was only of minimal importance when I went to one of the local hotels to see Alben Barkley, the Vice-President under Truman.

J.D. Early, who lived exactly one block down the street, was a pal of mine for many years. He was a true friend who was very easy to get along with. We used to like to go to the orange juice stand at Canal and Royal where they charged about a dime for a glass of fresh-squeezed juice and allowed you to reach into the bowl of peanuts and eat all you wanted; and we did eat. I liked oranges very much. I guess that they were too expensive for us to have at home very often, but we did have a lot of bananas. Whenever I had an orange, I squeezed it thoroughly and then added a little water to extend the drink. How I longed to have that little orange tree in our backyard blossom with fruit. I watered it and hoped for the best. When Daddy said that it would never produce, he was right. My hopes went down the drain.

When we were in our early teens, several of my friends, along with Albert and me, frequented the waterfront to see the ships that were docked. There we saw U.S. ships as well as those from England and

France (*Jeanne d'Arc*, for one). One of our ships I believe was the USS *Texas*, a battleship. On the decks of these ships, which were tied up to the dock, they showed movies for the crew. Even though we were able to view them, we couldn't hear the sound. Nevertheless, we felt like we were getting something for nothing. On my visits to the waterfront, I envied the sailors because I thought their life was very exciting. I dreamed that one day I would join the navy and go to sea. I envisioned the adventure element and didn't concentrate much on the hardship of life at sea. I always thought of myself as being an enlisted man. I never dreamed of becoming an officer.

When I was about thirteen years of age I became a tourist guide at the St. Louis Cathedral Church. There was no fixed pay. Instead, the old French Oblate Brother, who succeeded Brother Dionne, directed the activity and gave us our recompense. We got a slice of pie in the afternoon when the pie man stopped by (I loved raspberry), and he gave us 15 or 20 cents for a few hours of work. I would put this money in my pocket and head for home. I was a rich man. Then one day, about three days after I started this job, my father asked me what was I doing with my money. I told him that I was keeping it. "Oh no, your mother decides what you get. Give it to her." Unhappily, but promptly, I turned over my newly acquired riches to my mother. From then on I knew that she was the controller of my finances. She gave me a few nickels each time I worked and I was instructed to give my grandmother a bit of change, also. This whole episode is one for which I am very thankful. I learned a lesson early in life.

We made our time as tour guides exciting by exploring the upper reaches of the St. Louis Cathedral. We went up into the main steeple and even onto the catwalk above the church ceiling, where we traversed the walkway from the clock at the rear of the church on Chartres Street to the clock at the front near Royal Street. With one slip of the foot off of this catwalk we could have fallen through the plaster ceiling and then far below onto the church floor!

My father wanted Albert and me to go St. Aloysius High School, which was six and a half blocks away at Rampart and Esplanade Streets. Instead, we wanted to go to Jesuit High, which was several miles away at Carrollton and Banks Streets. I liked Jesuit particularly because they had the best football team, and I thought it would sound important to go there. My mother liked the Jesuit Fathers, so she sided with our selection and we got our way. My choice actually was a foolish one, because tuition was higher at Jesuit, the distance was farther, and I concluded in later years that the education at Aloysius was better. Fortunately, my brothers Joe, Mike, and Louis all attended St. Aloysius. Albert could have gotten a full scholarship at Aloysius if he were to play the bassoon, which he would have had to learn from scratch. But he did get a cut in tuition at Jesuit from $11 a month to $5 for playing trumpet in the band. Even though I also played in the band for four years, I wasn't given any reduction for this. Rather, I was granted a rate of $6 per month due to a competitive entrance exam that I took and therefore earned a partial scholarship.

My language curriculum at Jesuit High School consisted of four years of English, four years of Latin, and two years of French. The remaining studies were the usual basic requirements of religion, mathematics, history, etc.

Playing in the band was a wearisome task, because I wasn't too fond of it and the almost daily practices and participation in football game displays were too much for me. I played the clarinet, and my highest place in the band was only mediocre. During my third year at Jesuit, I contracted a violent outburst of a fungus on my hands and feet. It was a roaring case of athlete's foot. Many blisters appeared and spread due to the humidity and perspiration. I continued to attend all band practices after school even though I was in great distress one day. With swollen hands and feet, I was finally forced to stay home. It got so bad that two separate outbursts necessitated my missing school for 25 days. In one of these instances my feet were raw from Dr. Weilbaecher coming over and cutting the huge blisters open. I stayed awake all night listening to the clock strike every half hour. Boric acid soaks were about our only weapon, and they were practically useless.

I was deeply hurt year after year when the school failed to grant me a "letter"—the school emblem either on a sweater or jacket, or even just the emblem. Albert deserved and received adequate recognition in this regard and was even the captain of the band in his senior year. Around the time of the annual band concert, Daddy wanted me to enter the individual competition by playing a clarinet solo. He bought a reasonably simple piece of music for me, *Grand Fantasia*. I hated to disappoint him (and he didn't show his disappointment), but there was no way that I could have overcome my nervousness and performed in public. In private, I demonstrated to myself that I could play the music. But I knew that a private and a public performance were two different things.

I served Mass at the Jesuit Church (Church of the Immaculate Conception) on Baronne Street on Fridays when I was a sophomore and a junior at Jesuit High School. Venerable Brother Peter gave me twenty-five cents to buy a cup of coffee and a donut. This was the remuneration that all of the altar boys were given. And was it ever delicious to get this coffee and a doughnut at the Crystal hamburger stand on Royal and Canal Streets! Their hamburgers were outstanding, but that had to be on other days, because we were not allowed to eat meat on Fridays.

Sometimes Albert and I walked home from high school along the railroad tracks, picking up pieces of scrap iron, hoping to sell them. That never really amounted to anything because it was a losing proposition—the scrap iron was too heavy. Daddy gave us adequate carfare for our transportation, but sometimes we chose to save the money and walk instead. Occasionally, a friend drove us home from school, or sometimes we hitch-hiked.

De omni re scibili et quibusdam aliis—"Concerning everything knowable and a few other things besides"—referring to one who knows it all. I thought I was a big man when I decided to smoke at the age of eleven. Cigarettes were a penny apiece. Albert and I even smoked coffee grounds that we rolled up in bread paper. It surely smelled good. A couple of years later I decided to smoke a pipe, and when I was about 16 or so, I told my father that I smoked. Of course, my mother often queried me about this because she frequently told me that I smelled of smoke. Daddy "smoked" too, but not really. What he did mostly was chew on his Keep Moving cigars. Once in awhile he got a nice, more expensive Optimo cigar from someone as a gift.

When Daddy planned to explore some new enterprise, I was all excited. His venture into wine-making sounded good to me, but it seems that he deemed it a flop. However, I didn't! In any event, I don't recall that he ever repeated the process. When he made champagne and bottled it in beer bottles, he wrapped each bottle in newspaper and put them away to settle or age or something. When it came time to test the product, he was disappointed with its taste and didn't drink any more of it. Oops! He forgot to throw it away. So Albert and I gathered our friends in our makeshift clubhouse in the back yard and had champagne parties. I don't know if Daddy ever missed his supply.

When I graduated from Jesuit High School in June of 1941 at the age of 16 minus a few days, I had no idea what to do. Daddy suggested that I try to get a job at the Camera Mart at 322 Royal Street

Vestigia

in New Orleans. I walked the eight blocks to the store and spoke to Charlie Weber, one of the owners. Charlie told me that they didn't need any additional help, so I carried this message home to my father. His immediate response was, "Why don't you tell them that you will work for nothing?" Needless to say, I was absolutely shocked to hear this. Even though it sounded ridiculous, I went back to the store and followed his advice; I knew that he was much wiser than I. When I made this offer to Mr. Weber, he couldn't refuse—what did he have to lose? Pretty soon I was pushing a broom around and listening to camera talk.

Charlie thought that he was a good photographer, and I guess he was pretty fair, but there were two other men there who were really good—Roy Trahan and Stuart Lynn. It was obvious to me now that my dad wanted me to learn whatever I could from Roy Trahan and Stuart Lynn. And that I did. Soon I began making fifty cents a week, then a dollar or so, then ten dollars, and finally I got up to about thirteen dollars a week. I never considered what my percent increase in pay was, because I had started at nothing.

Roy had a stub for a left arm; I believe that he lost the rest of it while hopping off a train. He knew everything about photography and was an able and patient teacher. He later taught for years at Tulane University and was the official photographer for the football games. Stuart Lynn was a simple Kentucky man, about 30 years old or so, who was very anxious to become an expert photographer—I never really thought that he had to improve to get to that goal. It was an absolute pleasure to work with these two men. Charlie Weber came around only occasionally because he was an electrician full time. Annie Anderson, who had been a classmate of my sister Maxine, was another one of the owners. But this camera business wasn't a thriving enterprise, and this poor lady probably lost money. That was sad, too, because she was 28 years old and terribly crippled by arthritis. She always seemed to be leery of being duped.

One day, two men came into the shop and stood at the front counter near the door, so I went over to see what they wanted. They had a succinct request: Could I develop some pictures that they had taken at the local shipyard or naval base (I don't recall which)? I told them that if what they had was confidential, then I couldn't do it. They didn't stay long in the store, nor was it long before another well-dressed man came in and flashed a badge at me—"FBI." Somehow I managed not to faint.

31

He congratulated me on my refusal to process the film for the other men whom he had sent in to test me! A couple of months later, I was again approached by the FBI—two men this time. I've forgotten what the particulars were—they could still shock me, but not as badly. At that time we had a frequent visitor, Carlin Menge, probably our best customer, who made good money as the official photographer at Andrew Jackson Higgins Shipyard. Every PT boat that was built had to be photographed, and it was Carlin's job to do it. They also made the LCVP (Landing Craft Vehicle and Personnel). To some degree, therefore, our shop was connected with the shipyard. Perhaps that is the reason I was subjected to so much scrutiny by the FBI.

I became quite proficient at processing film and handling cameras of all varieties. My custom photo finishing was so good that even I liked it. One of our customers was Jacques Mossler, who I later learned was quite wealthy. He owned about six Savings and Loan companies throughout the South, in Louisiana, Texas, and Florida. Mr. Mossler was very happy with my work, and so I continued to make every effort to please him. He would bring in two rolls of 35 millimeter film to be processed and wanted it done in a certain tone. Each roll had thirty-six exposures on it, so his order took a fair amount of time.

I wanted to go to college, and Daddy and Mother surely agreed. I hope that the little money that I earned gave them some help in footing my bill. Since I was only sixteen, I didn't know what to study. Daddy provided the suggestion that I accepted: he said that I should consult the advisors at Loyola. It didn't take my advisor long to make his recommendation. He said that since I had been in an English-Latin curriculum at Jesuit, I should follow though with that plan at Loyola. Thus, I began night school five nights a week—via trolleys—studying Latin, English, religion, and algebra. The mathematics professor, Father Karl Maring, S.J., was outstanding and was almost as great as one of my teachers of high school math, Mr. Edward Gendron.

I can't mention Mr. Gendron's name without digressing and reflecting on my first day of class as a freshman in algebra at Jesuit High School, four years earlier in 1937. Most of the class was restless, wondering what it would be like to be in high school. Everyone was talking when Mr. Gendron walked into the room. Patiently, he said aloud, "Let's have quiet." Because he was a short man, no more than five feet five at best, there seemed to be little regard for his command. He looked around the room, and this time, he repeated his request a little

Vestigia

louder. He was quite patient. When his third entreaty got no results, he took action. Calmly he walked up to Carl Avrard, one of the vociferous students in the first row, and told him to stand up. When Carl stood, Mr. Gendron took him by the collar with one hand and used the other hand to pick him up by the seat of his pants. While holding Carl in a horizontal position, he brought him up to the blackboard and told him emphatically that he wouldn't tolerate that kind of behavior in his class. Of course, nothing could be more impressive to the students than such a show of strength and nothing more humiliating to Carl than to be so embarrassed in front of his peers. Needless to say, from then on, Mr. Gendron was firmly in charge of his class. We were impressed. Yet this story about one of my teachers is not over. The most significant attribute that he possessed beyond his teaching ability and his maintenance of discipline was his understanding. To illustrate this characteristic, I go back to later in the year, to an exam that we were taking in his class. I liked algebra and I comprehended it, but on this occasion I was on the verge of panic. I was confronted with a problem that perplexed me. The longer I sat and looked at it and looked at the clock, the more upset I became. I didn't know what to do. I thought I was going to flunk this test, and I couldn't bear to tell Daddy and Mother that I flunked. Right in the middle of the test, I walked up to Mr. Gendron's desk and told him that I didn't recognize that type of problem at all. It took this kind man just a moment to explain to me in private that this problem was one that was to be solved by cross multiplication, which he proceeded to exhibit. He picked me up from the depths and saved me! I was a little kid, perhaps the smallest in the class, and surely among the youngest, just a few months over twelve. The grammar school that I had come from was small and virtually unknown to my peers. Indeed, I felt diminished; I needed help! Many years later, when Mr. Gendron was in his eighties, I phoned him and thanked him. How can we ever forget such kindness?

As technology advances, we become more aware of the existence of toxic materials in our environment. What we did on a routine basis many years ago is absolutely unthinkable now. It was a common practice for us to play with mercury when I was a boy. The small bottle that we had in Daddy's workshop was probably a leftover from his days with chemistry. I was fascinated with the properties of this silvery liquid as I rolled it around from place to place and broke it up into many small globules. It also formed a slippery surface on silver coins. Asbestos was also very available for us to play with, and lead was the metal of choice to mold toy soldiers and Indians.

On December 7, 1941, as I sat in the hall at 1123 Royal, I heard a radio broadcast saying that the Japanese had bombed Pearl Harbor. That was very strange because I only knew of the Pearl River in Mississippi, and for the Japanese to have come all the way over to Mississippi to bomb some obscure river harbor was not very logical. It wasn't long before I found out that our major base in the Pacific had been all but wiped out. I was sixteen and a half years old then, when the excitement began that necessitated a military draft. One year later, when it was obvious that I would soon be eligible for the draft, even though I was a freshman at Loyola night school, my father suggested that I volunteer for the new V-1 Program that the navy was starting. This program was founded to provide naval officers with the necessary training in the minimum amount of time—the four-year program at Annapolis was far too slow for the immediate needs of the service. I followed my Dad's advice and went up to Canal and Camp Streets, I believe, to see Lieutenant Street. In no time at all, I was enlisted into the navy on January 28, 1943, with the instruction to report for active duty on July 1, 1943, to the newly formed unit of this program at Tulane University. For some reason, the program was later renamed V-12 instead of V-1.

In January of 1943, Mr. Mossler brought some film into the camera store for processing, but I told him that we couldn't take any more work because we were going out of business. He was distraught and didn't know what he would do about this problem. He then asked if I could do his work privately. When I told him that I myself didn't have any equipment at home to do his work, he offered to supply whatever I needed. He even drove up to my house one Sunday and picked me up to take me to his office. There he showed me the space that he would allocate to me and again said that all I had to do was tell him what equipment I needed. That whole situation just floored me, so I let him know that in a few days I would be making the transition from night school to full-time day school, and I had no idea what my schedule would be. I also pointed out the fact that his photography work wasn't sufficient in quantity to keep me busy. He wouldn't give up. "Work for me any time you're free, and fill in when you have no photographic work to do. You can do work in the office." Since I was now without a job and I had enrolled at Loyola full time, awaiting my date for re-

The family home at 1123 Royal Street.

porting to the navy, I thought it would be quite advantageous to work part time.

    For about seventeen dollars a week I worked in this fashion for Mr. Mossler while I attended Loyola. One of the duties that filled in my time between photo processing chores was the handling of office supplies in the two-story Savings and Loan building on Canal Street. A freight elevator had been designed for the previous owner to carry an automobile up to the second-level parking area, but since the building was now serving another purpose, the elevator had a different use. We used it now for freight and, in particular, for such things as office supplies. One afternoon, I used the large door and placed several hundred pounds of various paper forms on the elevator floor. When everything was loaded, I proceeded to pull the control cord to start our upward ascent. As we began to rise, a strange thing happened—part of the open-top car went up and part didn't. The elevator platform rose and fell as the unit twisted diagonally, and the part that refused to go just inched upward instead, poking stabbing gouges into the shaft wall. As I was being thrust back and forth on this pulsing floor, I was beset by a massive amount of strewn paper. A fearsome noise added to the turmoil. I couldn't stop this wild beast, and when I looked up and saw the huge steel girder that was actually the top of the cage twisting violently, I decided that it was time to take drastic action. I had to get out before the floor level of the elevator got up to the height of the door lintel; if I didn't, I'd be trapped! I made my decision and decided to jump from my churning platform about eight feet to the ground. The elevator continued its violent ascent up the shaft, poking and gouging its way diagonally. After I got away from this menace, I went into the office area adjacent to the elevator. The frightened workers had no idea of what was going on; they were just scared. I told them that the elevator had gotten out of control. Soon the violent racket stopped. Later the company management sheepishly acknowledged that a janitor had failed to hang an "Out of Order" sign on the elevator to indicate it was off its track.

    When I thought I deserved a raise, I asked my immediate boss about it and found out that even his boss couldn't handle my request. Since I was hired by Mr. Mossler, I had to go directly to him. When he came back into town, I went into his office and spoke to him. He mulled it over for a few seconds and then conceded to a raise—just a few cents, at that. Many years later, I read in the paper that he had been murdered. Later, this murder was the subject of a paperback publication.

About this time in my life there was a dramatic change in my outlook toward music. I developed an appreciation for opera, and I became particularly engrossed in the clarinet. I paid to go to operas, and I even took dates to these performances. Daddy taught me what he knew about the clarinet and then suggested that any further study should be with a specialist. Mr. Giuffre, who had previously taught Maxine on our metal Penzel Mueller clarinet, was my choice. He was really, really good. I paid two dollars per lesson, which was supposed to be for a half hour, but they were usually much longer than that. I was disappointed, however, when he couldn't accompany me on his clarinet because of his heart condition. The best way to sum up my progress was in his own words: "Mr. Levy, when you play, your execution is fine; your timing is fine; but your tone…your tone…is like—it's like you stepped on the head of a dog." That criticism really rocked me to my foundation. I came home and told my father and asked him if I shouldn't quit. I'll never forget his calm, wise advice: "Son, you go back to Mr. Giuffre and continue taking lessons. When the day comes that he doesn't complain about your tone, then you make him pay to hear you play." From then on, I practiced my clarinet every day for hours at a time. I must have driven everybody nuts. But the day never arrived when Mr. Giuffre had to pay to hear me.

Daddy enjoyed playing the piano, and I knew that he enjoyed it even more when I would ask him if I could accompany him with my clarinet. I don't know how he was able to put up with my playing, because he was a very fine musician and I was pretty bad. Nevertheless, he never lost patience with me. When I wanted a new wooden clarinet to replace the old metal one, Daddy and Mother purchased a beautiful new Conn instrument, which I guess cost about $125. I enjoyed the saxophone, too, and tried my hand at it. My failure to play the clarinet well has always been a big disappointment to me. I worked hard at it, but at least I enjoyed it.

One of the clarinet selections that I practiced for many hours was *La Sonnambula*. It was several pages long and encompassed numerous cadenzas. I thought that if I were ever able to conquer this piece, I would have achieved my goal. Frequently, Daddy accompanied me on the piano and, again, his patience with me was masterful. I guess that, after many hours, I must have improved, but I was far from my goal.

Chapter Four

Wartime

As scheduled, on July 1, 1943, I reported to Tulane University on Freret Street in New Orleans to begin my military service. The navy had taken over various portions of the university campus and housed most of the V-12 contingent—1,200 of us—in the revamped gym. Those were crowded quarters in which I lived for two semesters from July 1943 until March 1944. I blamed my poor grades on the living conditions and the study locale. We had to turn in at night at about nine o'clock unless we walked all the way over the campus to what was called late study. There, if we signed in, we could study until about 10:30. This was not too profitable, however, because it was a long walk across the campus for just a little more study time. Additionally, I was a poor sleeper, and we had to rise at six in the morning and immediately proceed outdoors to run several laps around the field.

How comical it was one morning when we were running and the fog was so dense that only our bobbing heads were visible above the fog bank. Some fellows ducked below, into the fog, and hid in the bushes. In this manner, they skipped a lap here and there. During this exercise one morning, I fell over abruptly when my left knee locked up. Later, in the examination room at Sick Bay, they diagnosed the problem as some minor ailment that I believe they called water on the knee and sent me on my way. Fortunately, this situation did not recur exactly the same way, but I did have periodic distress and swelling thereafter. Finally, one day they decided to x-ray my knee. It was determined that I had a calcified haematoma that required surgery. The doctors, Prieto and Kuhn, provided the care for all of the naval personnel. For a few days I was confined to Touro Infirmary on Camp Street. After proper recuperation, I was as good as new. As soon as I got out of the hospital, I had a date with my nurse.

The first thing that we learned in the navy was their own peculiar terminology. It seems like nothing kept its regular name, but, rather, it was given some odd designation or pronunciation. Pieces of rope or cable with pulleys were called tackle, but, of course, it was not pronounced "tack-el," it was called "take-el." Walls are bulkheads; the floor is the deck; the ceiling is the overhead; steps are called ladders. The most confusing terminology, however pertained to personnel. Whereas the army, Marine Corps, and air force have certain names for their rank, the navy uses some of these names but places their positions at a different level. For example, an army First Lieutenant is a Lieutenant Junior Grade in the navy; an army Captain is a navy Lieutenant, and an army Colonel is a navy Captain. Additionally, whoever is in charge of a ship, no matter what his rank, is called "Captain." And whoever is in charge of deck hardware on a ship is called the "First Lieutenant." In order to convey proper respect for your vessel, it is important to remember that any vessel that can be transported on board another vessel is called a "boat"; otherwise it is a "ship." It is disrespectful to refer to a ship as a boat. One huge exception to this rule pertains to submarines. For some strange reason, a submarine is always called a "boat."

 I didn't have sufficient credits in March of 1944 to graduate, but since the navy had provided me with a full year of college and they needed officers, they shipped me off to pre-midshipmen school at Asbury Park, New Jersey. That was a fancy name for a holding facility. This assignment was necessary because the midshipmen schools were full at the time. I loved the train ride to New Jersey; it was thrilling to travel through the snow, and it added to my never-ending love of steam engines. The complex at Asbury Park consisted of two hotels surrounded by a high wooden fence. These hotels were right in the boardwalk area of this resort city near New York. For ten weeks we drilled and cleaned up the place. The food was modest and sparse—one helping only at mealtime. I supplemented my evening meal with O'Henry candy bars. Our room with one bath, in the Berkeley Carteret Hotel, was over-loaded because there were six of us in it. We were so close to the ocean in this "luxury" hotel that I heard the waves all night. I wasn't used to that noise, and it bothered me. Later on, it became music to my ears. The other hotel that the navy used was the Monterey, which was not supposed to be as swanky because it was somewhat removed from the beach and appeared a bit older.

 This base of ours was a dual facility. We shared it with the British, who ran a radar school—which was very secret at the time. It was a while before I found out what that revolving antenna was. It seemed strange to me when I looked up at the top of one of the buildings and saw the American flag flying side by side with the British flag.

Vestigia

Every Saturday, in Asbury Park, we had Captain's Inspection around noon or so. The delays during this ceremony seemed interminable while we held our wooden rifles. I never could understand why it was necessary to keep us in ranks, waiting for one man to decide to inspect us.

It was in June when my tour of duty in New Jersey was over and I was placed with many others on a troop train bound for Chicago. At the first announcement, my name was not on the list of those selected to depart. Later on, a revised list was issued, and I was overjoyed to find out that now I had been included. On this train we had makeshift bunks three deep and very close together. This was about a nine-hundred-mile trip and obviously not too comfortable. But it was a train, and I liked trains.

Chicago had two alternating locales for midshipmen classes. They would graduate about four months apart. Abbott Hall was one of these places, and Tower Hall was the other; both of them were a part of Northwestern University. Abbott Hall was sort of a permanent structure, whereas Tower Hall, my home, was a recent takeover by the navy. It was a twelve-story health facility right by the old water tower at 820 Tower Court near Pearson, Rush, and Chicago Streets. Here at my new address on Tower Court, my room number was 712; I shared this room with seven other men. Ironically, at a later date that year, I was to be stationed aboard a ship that bore the same number, 712.

Every Sunday night, upon return from liberty, we were compelled to attend church services, either Catholic or Protestant. I don't think there was any special consideration for Jews. We Catholics were marched around the corner to the Holy Name Cathedral for Rosary and Benediction. I had already been to Mass in the morning, and in this era there was no afternoon Mass.

We had liberty every afternoon around suppertime, and the popular thing to do was drop in at a neighborhood bar for a beer. With such a short time for this, it caused excessive crowding in the bar. One of my roommates and I found the perfect solution: there was another bar very near that no one else had seemed to find; we were the only two sailors there. One day, I told another one of my buddies about this place, and he proceeded to walk me over to the bulletin board to read the notice that alerted us to the fact that this place was out of bounds! I considered myself fortunate to learn before it was too late.

Since we had to complete our studies in about ninety days, before being commissioned, the environment was rigorous. Officers who were commissioned after such training were often referred to as "Ninety-Day Wonders." We studied navigation, ordnance, and seamanship. For the latter, we used a book that we had first seen at Tulane, *Knight's Modern Seamanship*. For navigation, we had Bowditch's venerable text, along with various Navy Hydrographic Office (HO) Publications, such as HO 214 and HO 211. Several months later I met the author of the latter book. This man was Commander Arthur A. Ageton, whom I believe was at one time the Executive Officer of the battleship USS *Washington* when it was involved in a collision. I believe both he and the skipper of the battlewagon were removed from their jobs and received some kind of demotion.

While in midshipmen school, we had to take a three-day training trip at sea on Lake Michigan. Just as we were preparing to go to the dock to board the USS *Wilmette*, I was called to the Duty Office for an extremely rare phone call. I was heartbroken to hear from home that Albert had been shot down over Germany and was missing in action. Now I was to spend the next three days in a brand new environment with this catastrophic revelation on my mind!

Lake Michigan was rough. It absolutely surprised me as I lay on the deck of the ship, which was my "bunk." I never thought that an inland body of water could be so wild. I felt like I was in elite company when I was taken to the bridge to see radar in action. I guess I would say that it was on this trip I proved to myself that not only could I endure the sea, but I liked it. My boyhood thoughts, as I used to watch the sailors on the ships by the dock in New Orleans, came to fruition. I was now one of them. We also made other ventures on the lake as part of our training. We used civilian craft that the navy had procured in some fashion and termed them YPs, which stood for Yard Patrol. We formed "convoys," we maneuvered and performed various drills.

On September 14, 1944, I received my commission as an Ensign in the U.S. Naval Reserve from Admiral Randall Jacobs, the Chief of Naval Personnel, at Navy Pier in Chicago while my proud father and mother looked on. They had come over from Indianapolis where there was a convention of the National Catholic Evidence Guild. I found it incredible that at the age of nineteen I was a commissioned officer in the navy. My father was anxious to see the first salute that would be rendered. Ceremoniously, there was always a gathering of enlisted men outside waiting to give the first salute to an officer. This is because it is customary to award a dollar to the first man who salutes a newly commissioned officer. As badly as my father had wanted to receive a commission himself in his youth, he was even more pleased to see his son receive one. I realized this joy myself in later life as I witnessed my own children being granted their degrees, graduate degrees, and certifications.

After the commissioning ceremony and formal dance on the north side of Chicago at the Aragon Ballroom, I went by train with Daddy and Mother to St. Louis. There we visited Muriel at 5341 Emerson Avenue, where she took care of young girls who were variously diminished. I was so tired from the previous excitement that I fell asleep as some kind soul drove us on a sightseeing tour through Forest Park. I couldn't tell you a thing about it.

Then, by Illinois Central Railroad, we proceeded to New Orleans, where I was to spend two weeks on leave. While at home, a mail truck drove up to our door when I happened to be on the front gallery. I could see down through the windshield as I stood directly overhead. I spied a document with two large stars on it and immediately I knew it was from the government. I raced to the door, got the telegram, and gave it to Beryl, Albert's wife, who lived with us. A weird sense of relief came over me as I learned that Albert had survived but was now a prisoner of the German government. I found that to be strange terminology.

Now, with that gloom over my head, I left by train for San Francisco in accordance with my orders. I was to proceed to the ComAdComPhibPac (Commander Administrative Command Amphibious Forces Pacific Fleet). When asked in school to give my preference for duty assignment, I had requested capital ships (combat vessels), particularly destroyers. My orders, nevertheless, and typically so, were at this time for our most needed forces, the amphibious navy, which consisted of the LST (Landing Ship Tanks), LSD (Landing Ship Dock), LSM (Landing Ship Medium), and LCI (Landing Craft Infantry). One of these types of vessels would be my ultimate assignment.

When I arrived in San Francisco in the latter part of September 1944, I reported to the Federal Building on Market Street. I was assigned to the Bachelor Officers' Quarters (BOQ) in the Alexander Hamilton Hotel on Leavenworth and O'Farrell Streets. My instructions were to report in every day while awaiting assignment. Since this hotel was only three blocks away, I decided to forego a taxi and walk this short distance. After carrying my baggage for a block and a half, I realized that this three-block journey was pretty stiff, because it was up a steep hill with a forty-pound load. I wasn't going to take a cab now for just one and a half blocks, but I regretted my earlier decision to walk. This was my introduction to the hills of San Francisco.

Each day I phoned in to the Federal Building, and when I was told I had no assignment yet, I went sightseeing and in general just killed time.

One day in early October, the time had come at last. I was told to go to a certain address downtown and be ready to ship out by plane—that was all I knew.

After reporting to the given address, I was driven to the waterfront and put aboard a navy Coronado Flying Boat. Wow! Was that ever exciting. I was now going to make the first flight of my life to some unknown place. After being squeezed aboard a "hollowed out" (no amenities) seaplane, we taxied back and forth in the San Francisco Bay until we could rough up the water enough to break the capillary attraction and lift off. Pearl Harbor, we were told, was our destination in this four-engine, triple-tail giant whose speed was less than 200 miles an hour. All night we flew in this cold plane as I pondered the information that someone had given me before the flight. I was told that the last trip had been beset with an engine failure. We were supposed to take solace in the fact that this previous trip was able to be completed with the remaining three engines.

Well, we made it, and I was now in "Pearl" to spend a few days awaiting assignment to the next amphibious ship that needed an officer. It seemed strange to me that there weren't any obvious scars of the blistering attack that had taken place here almost three years earlier. If you knew where to look, you could find signs of the sunken ships, but this was a beautiful place; this was the island of Oahu.

I spent some time in the Officer's Club, where I watched the poker games. This naval base was a center for the re-assignment of personnel returning from the war zone; most were to return to the States. There were many participants in the card games, and the stakes were quite high. With the frequent betting and raising of bets, I had difficulty estimating the value of the pot. When I saw fifty- and hundred-dollar bills being thrown onto the table, I wondered how long it had taken for these men to save that kind of money. It was obvious that some of these officers had spent a lot of time overseas and had saved a lot of money, only to lose it at the gambling table. I wondered what life had been like for these men who had gone before me into that vast expanse of the Pacific.

Vestigia

Having spent my training time in Chicago in Room 712 of Tower Hall while at midshipmen's school, where was I now to be assigned? None other than LST-712 (Landing Ship Tanks).

The crew of the LST received me warmly, but I felt like the greenhorn that I was. Already they had taken this ship down the Mississippi to New Orleans for commissioning and then on shakedown cruise to Panama City, Florida, and back to New Orleans. From there they had gone through the Panama Canal to Pearl Harbor. If the crew had been new when they came aboard, they were certainly veterans now. I was the only rookie.

We soon departed from Pearl Harbor in a westerly direction, heading for Banika, an island in the Russell Island Group in the South Pacific. My fellow officers, all older than I, enjoyed my excitement over the beautiful blue of the Pacific. I was used to the brown, muddy Mississippi, and Lake Michigan hadn't left any special impression on me except that it was terribly rough at times.

About two weeks later we arrived at Banika, and it was generally uneventful, except that we caught fire when some welders outfitted our hull with pontoon brackets. The heat caused an internal compartment on the inner side of the ship's skin to burst out in the flames of the kapok life jackets stored there.

In waters like this where there is a coral bottom, we could usually see our own ship's anchor lying on the seafloor, even when the depth was over one hundred feet.

An LST is about 328 feet in length, has a 50-foot beam, and displaces about 2000 tons. It has two diesel main engines of about 1000 horsepower each, which generate a maximum of 300 propeller revolutions per minute. The ship can achieve approximately 11 knots. When ballasted for sea it would draw 8 feet forward and 14 feet aft. We usually carried a crew of about nine commissioned officers and about 120 enlisted men. There was space for about 200 troops and two pontoon rafts, along with numerous tanks, trucks, jeeps, and other cargo. There were three auxiliary engines used to generate electrical power. When at sea, two of these engines would always be on line. We burned about 2000 gallons of fuel each day at sea and carried a total of about 180,000 gallons, as I recall. We had about 80,000 gallons of fresh water, and, when necessary, we could generate, by evaporation of sea water, about 2000 gallons of potable water per day. We seldom used this watermaking facility, because it was laborious to have to clean the evaporators. They became caked with residue from the evaporation process.

We also carried two LCVP (Landing Craft Vehicle Personnel), one each on our port and starboard davits. These diesel-powered boats had a bow ramp and were capable of carrying thirty-six men or one vehicle with a few men. Their speed was about fourteen knots.

An LST is a strange ship. It is designed to ride up onto the sandy beach where it can unload its cargo. If the gradient of the beach is such that a "dry ramp" cannot be achieved, then you are assured by the shallow forward draft that any unloading will be done into a minimum depth of water. One time we had a navy "four striper" (Captain) aboard, and he was commenting to me about this strange aspect of the LST. He said that he had always been taught never to let his ship go aground, and now he was riding on one that reversed all of this philosophy. We are taught to bring LSTs onto the beach. One other situation that I never mentioned to him was the possibility of losing an anchor. In "his" navy, you never lost your anchor. But in the amphibious navy, you sometimes did. I know that to be a fact, because we did that very thing. When we reported loss of our stern anchor to the task force commander, it didn't seem to generate any unusual response—we were told to grapple for it. In a reasonable amount of time, we were successful in locating the lost anchor and soon brought it back aboard.

It was Commander Arthur A. Ageton's plight to be assigned to the amphibious forces in the Pacific Fleet. That is how I met him in the middle of the ocean. At that time during the war, while our ship, along with numerous others, was "lying to"—stationary at sea—I was summoned to Ageton's flagship, an LCI (Landing Craft Infantry). I was the Stores Officer on my LST, and a few of my men and I went by LCVP (Landing Craft Vehicle and Personnel) and joined other men for a meeting with the Commander on the deck of his ship. When he looked down at me and saw my men in fatigues, he immediately asked whose men were these who were out of uniform. When I 'fessed up, he chewed me out by telling me that I should have read his FlotCom Memo (Flotilla Commander Memorandum "umpty ump"). He expected us to be in regular uniform (dungarees) out here in the Pacific in the Ulithi Atoll near the island of Yap...

During November and December of 1944, we tooled around the islands going to Guadalcanal, the Florida Islands, Tulagi, Manus, Emirau, and other places. Finally, we loaded up with troops, tanks, and vehicles at Hollandia, New Guinea; from there we went to Sansapor, New Guinea, to stage for the forthcoming invasion. While in that har-

Vestigia

bor one night, I saw my first Japanese plane. It came over at dusk and was immediately sought after by the radar-controlled spotlights that the Marines had on the beach. All of our ships opened fire. We thought that our cause was lost when the pilot got refuge in a cloud. It wasn't long, however, before the cloud exploded into a brilliant red as the shells hit their mark. This plane was also being pursued by one of our own P-61 Black Widow night fighter planes. As I recall, the intense gunfire of adjacent ships also brought down our own fighter plane. Until this close encounter, I had never realized that my knees would shake in such a situation. I was scared.

When it was time for us to depart for the invasion of Luzon, we proceeded up the west coast of the Philippines. It was frightening to know that we were in hostile waters and always getting closer to battle. It was so comforting to us whenever we could see our own capital ships on the horizon, protecting us. The presence of P-51 American fighter planes was very assuring. It not only made us feel safe, but we also felt very important.

At the sound of General Quarters (GQ), when every man must report to his assigned battle station, we had to don our life jackets and helmets; additionally, each officer had to wear his holster and pistol. All of these items were kept close to our bunk. Often we had to don this gear hurriedly, and we didn't have much time to prepare.

Every morning and evening, whether at sea or in a harbor, we were harassed by Japanese planes. One of these times in the Philippines, a kamikaze came after us. All of the ships in the convoy began to fire at it. Our ship was directly in the path of fire from one of our own ships, and we were an obvious target for this Japanese suicide pilot. He chose not to attack us; instead, he passed us at mast height, close enough for me to see his face. I was thankful that he chose to bypass us but saddened to see what he did to a Liberty ship ahead. First he dropped a bomb on it, then looped around and dove into the ship and set it afire. I turned to one of the Sea Bee officers that we had aboard and asked him, "What do you do in a case like this?" He calmly replied, "When in danger or in doubt, run in circles, yell and shout." The words "Sea Bee" came from the letters "C" and "B," which meant Construction Battalion. All men in this operation had signed up with the navy to pursue their particular talents in the area of construction, which was vitally needed in the many bases that were to be built in the islands.

On our way up the west coast of the Philippines to Lingayen Gulf, we had our persistent sunrise and sunset air raids by kamikazes. Once, as we generated a smokescreen while we were underway, a Japanese plane was heard overhead. I caught sight of it in a clearing of the smoke. Soon thereafter, LST-912, on our starboard beam about 700 yards away, opened fire with one of its 40-millimeter guns. I saw the Japanese plane go directly toward that ship, apparently using the tracer fire for guidance. It then crashed into the ship and killed the gun crew. It was terrible.

About this same time, it was decided that while we were underway, it was not a good practice to generate a smokescreen because it sometimes made it difficult for us to see where we were going. Nevertheless, when the enemy is overhead, you make exceptions. My station for General Quarters was at the stern, right by the smoke generator. During one of the air raids when it was decided to make smoke, the machine caught fire. It was ironic that here we were trying to hide ourselves, and instead we were actually providing illumination. Fearful of the heat that was being generated by the fire beneath a gun tub stocked with 40-millimeter ammunition in it, we threw many of these rounds overboard.

On January 9, 1945, we participated in the invasion of Lingayen Gulf on the northern coast of Luzon, the largest of the Philippine Islands. The massive force that we assembled included General MacArthur. It was one of the largest amphibious invasions in history, second in size only to the Normandy invasion on June 6, 1944, in Europe.

One of my collateral duties aboard ship was the housing of military officers whom we transported, along with their troops and cargo. In each of the staterooms of our own ship's officers, there were additional bunks for other officers we carried. Whenever we were about to load up, I checked the roster for the possibility of a chaplain. Only once or maybe twice did we have a Catholic priest aboard. When we did have a chaplain of any denomination, I always made sure that he was assigned to the stateroom of a certain officer whom I deemed was in most need of conversion. In due time, this officer became aware of my ploy and asked for a change in policy.

Whenever it was a Sunday and we were in a harbor, I tried to research the potential there for church services. I would have our signalman contact all the ships asking if they had a chaplain aboard. When my efforts were successful, I arranged for a "Church Party." On

Vestigia

schedule, one of our boats carried our personnel to the other ship. In that manner we tried to have both Catholic Mass and Protestant services for the crew. I don't recall ever seeing a rabbi out in the Pacific.

When we were on another ship for church services, and time permitted, I'd go below deck on some of these ships in order to visit the areas that had been out of bounds to me as a boy when I went aboard naval vessels in the Mississippi.

On Sundays when were we at sea and there was no chaplain aboard, if the opportunity presented itself, I tried to conduct some type of church service. We would say the Rosary and I would read the Gospel. Many times while we were at sea in convoy (we always traveled in convoy), I received General Absolution from a priest on one of the neighboring ships, according to the policy he had presented to the convoy before sailing. He had said that whenever General Quarters was sounded (enemy contact was imminent), all we had to do was make an Act of Contrition and he would impart General Absolution to all of us no matter how far away we were.

There was a mailbox on the ship that would be filled every day with outgoing letters. No mail, however, was allowed to leave the ship until it was censored. The officers had the job of reading every letter and censoring it. We were given a rubber stamp and had to affix our initials within the imprint. Everybody knew what was allowed to be written and what was forbidden. Nevertheless, I believe that some of the men enjoyed having their mail go to their family with sections having been cut out. When time would allow, we would rather give a letter back to someone to re-write rather than having to cut holes in it. Days often went by without any opportunity to offload our mail. I used to read stacks and stacks of personal mail; I hated doing it. As far as our incoming mail was concerned, that was something else; it was very spasmodic. We would go for days and days without any. Then one day, in some port that you would least expect, there it would be—sacks and sacks of mail. Sometimes it would be damp, crumpled, or pristine. Our crew received many boxes of crumbled cookies. But no matter what shape it was in, mail was a real treasure. In order to maintain continuity, letters from my home were numbered. I remembered the time that Daddy was very sick with a high fever. That was the time that I couldn't bear to read the letters sequentially. Instead, I immediately reached for the most recent letter, which fortunately told of his recovery.

After we had spent some time between the various island groups and seen scores of men who had been overseas for many months, we learned to distinguish immediately who the old-timers were. Those who had been there the longest were the "yellowest." Because malaria was a major problem for all of us, we were put on a regimen of Atabrine as a preventive measure. I assume that it worked well in preventing malaria, but it surely made us turn yellow. In due time, after we had gotten off of the medicine, everyone returned to their normal appearance, but I have no idea if this medicine ever had any effect on our systems.

Every time we entered a new geographical area, we were inoculated against the diseases that were considered to be most prevalent in that locale. We were given so very many of these shots that it is impossible to recall all of them. On some occasions, these inoculations were repeated either because of doubtful quality of the serum used or as a booster necessary because of the preponderance of the feared disease in a given area. I was therefore immune to so many diseases that I almost felt immune to death itself. Despite this, I harbored a ridiculous—yet realistic—fear as I walked along the beach on numerous islands and heard the falling coconuts plop to the ground from their great heights. How would my mother feel if she ever got the report that her son was killed in action by a falling coconut?

OKINAWA INVASION:

(Statistical data in this section is taken from page 20 of the November/December 1999 issue of *LST Scuttlebutt*, published by the United States LST Association, P.O. Box 167438, Oregon, Ohio 43616.)

Okinawa is a long, slim island (60 miles long and 9 miles wide) in the Nansei Shoto group of the Ryukyu Islands, lying about 350 miles southwest of Japan. My LST participated in the invasion there on Easter Sunday, April 1, 1945. The fighting lasted until June 22, 1945. Okinawa is mountainous, volcanic, and covered thickly with vegetation. Most importantly, it was littered with underground grave sites marked by concrete protuberances a few feet above the ground—about 435,000 Japanese, Chinese, and other Asians.

Vestigia

The Japanese fortified this island with 100,000 men of the 32nd Army and about 3,500 men of a special navy landing force sometimes called the Japanese Marines. Additionally, there were about 7,000 militarized civilians and another 20,000 men in the territorial militia. Waiting for our attack was the Shuri Line and the feared explosive boats and the kamikaze planes.

Operation Iceberg, as it was called, was the detailed plan of Admiral Richmond Kelly Turner. It consisted of a total of 1,657 ships, including 343 LSTs of Task Force 51 of the U.S. Fifth Fleet, of which I was a member. The British also furnished three task groups and five small aircraft carriers.

We carried elements of the First Armored Amphibious Marines under Colonel Metzger on our ship. They were a part of Major General Roy Geiger's (not on our ship) Third Marine Corps. He had three divisions totaling 81,165 men.

The U.S. Navy had 318 capital ships in the Okinawa invasion. There were ten battleships, nine cruisers, twenty-three destroyers, and one hundred seventy-seven gunboats. These ships pounded the beaches for five days before the landing.

Initially, there was no resistance to our invasion except on the outer periphery of our array of ships, which were attacked by kamikazes. Then, as time drew on, the Japanese fought back with such fury that I was fearful of ever surviving. On one particular day while we were in the harbor, I saw the fierce battle over our heads that resulted in 400 Japanese planes being shot down (I learned of the number from a later news source). There was flack everywhere from our ships, and parts of planes were flying around all over the sky.

A total of 133 of our ships were hit by kamikazes, plus five by mines, five by suicide boats, and three hit by coastal batteries. Out of this total, 34 of our ships were sunk, 26 others were scrapped or decommissioned, and 40 others were damaged—a total of 100 ship casualties. The total naval casualties amounted to 9,896 men, of which about 4,907 were killed or missing.

For the Okinawa initial landing, along with the First Armored Amphibious Marines, we carried a lot of gasoline and bombs. The marines left our ship by LVT (Landing Vehicle Tracked) at the precise appointed time for the invasion. Then, like all of the amphibious ships, we had to drop anchor off shore and await the call to come into the beach to unload cargo. Our captain was quite concerned during numerous air raids, having gasoline and bombs on board and waiting to be called in to the beach to unload. So Luther Wells and I went ashore by LVT at dusk to see the Beach Master who was in charge of calling ships in to unload. As we walked together down the beach, visible by the lights that were strung on wooden posts placed in the sand, we heard an announcement over the bullhorn. There was a report of an impending paratroop attack by the Japanese. Because of this threat, all unloading operations were to cease immediately; no boats were to move along the beach, and all illumination was extinguished. Also, in order to prevent infiltration by the enemy, it was now required that all personnel issue a password challenge to whomever they met. Since I was the Stores Officer aboard our ship and Wells was the Communications Officer, I was sure that he would know the password. Rather frightened in the blackness of night and eeriness of this situation, I asked Wells, "What's the password?" I surely didn't want to hear his reply: "I don't know."

Down the beach we continued, fearful that we would meet someone and be challenged. There in the dark lurked a shadow, and soon it became a man. "What's the password?" I asked him. "What's it worth to you?" he said. Now I was really puzzled. Was he challenging me with the correct password, or was he trying to be funny? As we continued talking, I realized that he presented no threat. It seems we were not the only ones who were ignorant of the password. When we reached the Beach Master and relayed the message that our Captain had given us, he then gave us permission to return to our ship. We wasted no time in getting out of there. We never did find out what the password was.

It was not long before we were called to beach our ship and begin unloading. Hot shrapnel from the Japanese shore batteries hit the deck of our ship and gave evidence of our precarious plight.

Each of our two invasions earned a star for us on our Pacific Area Campaign ribbon. For weeks thereafter we were busy traveling back and forth between the islands, ferrying troops and supplies back up to the front. I remember very well one of these trips during the Philippine invasion. We had brought replacement troops back to the initial drop-off spot and found out then that most of the others that we had transported here before, some of whom I had gotten to know, had been wiped out.

We had constant reminders of the cruelty of war and how close we came to disaster. During one of our trips, our Duty Officer, Elmer Matson, let us know in the morning that on his midnight watch, a torpedo had gone right under our ship. That was one of the advantages in having a ship of shallow draft. Then again, because of our weird configuration of blunt nose, flat bottom, and shallow draft, we were an extremely rough riding vessel. During rough seas we would bounce around, pitch, roll, creak, and groan. Many was the time that I just knew we weren't going to make it.

I found it particularly difficult to get accustomed to the non-routine sleep hours that we had attendant to our duties. Then, too, there was the frequent interruption in those hours by air raids. It was also an emotional drain to shoulder the heavy responsibility of "standing underway watches" during wartime in the dead of night in convoys that were totally dark. Unless there was a moon to help us, all we had was the light from the stars and the waterline illumination provided by the disturbance of the plankton in the sea. The underway watch about which I speak is a unique situation. Here it is that the Officer of the Deck, the O.D., on rotation had to spend four hours at a time in complete command of the ship. He gave orders by voice tube to the wheelhouse where the quartermaster was steering the ship. Via this same means, he gave orders to the engine room to adjust the speed as necessary. It was in this manner that station-keeping in proper convoy position was kept. When convoy course changes were necessary, it was a challenging endeavor to turn your own ship at the correct spot to come out of the maneuver in proper station position—400 yards astern and 700 yard abeam of adjacent ships. Close ship positioning was necessary in order to keep our convoy tight as a defense against submarine attacks. When I thought of the 120-plus men in our own crew and the sometime 200 or so army personnel aboard, as well as the value of the ship and the cargo we carried, I wondered how a nineteen-year-old kid like me could handle such responsibility. At night, this station-keeping within the convoy had to be done by the OD with the use of binoculars alone as a guide to distance, because radar was in its infancy and the S0 10 model that we had was inadequate and very prone to failure. Additionally, an LST has an awful lot of inertia and is thus difficult to keep in proper position. Most of the time while we were underway, we ran our screws (propellers) at about 280 shaft rpm. Since 300 rpm is the maximum that we could go, it is easy to see that we didn't have much reserve power to catch up if we lagged behind. We called the LST a "Large Slow Target."

We frequently had rain squalls and heavy weather. Fortunately, it wasn't until much later, after the war, that we had the additional problem of cold weather. The tropics, where we operated, were always pleasantly warm. Therefore, the frequent rain squalls were no great problem. Heavy weather was something else.

No matter what I ate, I never seemed to gain weight. I was always about 138 pounds. This era of dehydrated potatoes and eggs, along with weevil-infested bread, was no time to try to put on weight. I just wanted to survive. I sent a regular allotment, automatically deducted from my pay, to my mother. My base pay amounted to $150 per month plus an overseas bonus of $15. I seem to recall, too, that officers had to pay a monthly mess bill.

Luther Wells, thirteen years my senior, had his room just across the passageway from me. All officers lived in staterooms that, when you consider the situation, were quite comfortable and privileged quarters. Luther, an engaging personality, was an artist who had worked for *Harper's Bazaar* and *Ladies Home Journal* magazines. He with his sketchpad and I with my Zeiss Ikonta camera would trudge wherever we were allowed to compile pictorial data. Our skipper, Stan Jolivette, was very generous in allowing us to go ashore and explore; we would furnish him with pictures on our return. It was not without difficulty that I was able to do so, because procuring the chemicals to develop these photos was not easy.

One time when our ship was in Olongapo on the coast of Luzon in the Philippines, we hitched a ride on an LCI to go the eighty or so miles to Manila via Bataan and Caballo. I was amazed to see the vast number of sunken ships protruding halfway out of the water in Manila Bay. Luther and I found a place to spend the night in the crew's quarters of the LCI where they had moored in the Bay. Another escapade was our trip ashore once in the Philippines to get ship's mail, only to return to our anchorage to find that the ship had moved. After circling around for some period of time, it was not long before darkness began to settle in. Lo and behold, the nightly Japanese air raid was upon us! Here we were out in a 36-foot LCVP and no place to go, just hoping that no falling flak would hit us. We pulled up alongside an LST, and Luther went aboard to ask them if we could spend the night on the ship. For some reason or other, he was told that our officers, Luther and I, could go aboard but that they couldn't accommodate the enlisted men we had with us (maybe two or three). That was it—we decided that if we all

Vestigia

couldn't go aboard, then we would just tie our boat up to the side of the LST and sleep in our open boat. That's how we spent the night, using life jackets for pillows. We had C rations in our emergency supplies to help us.

While we were anchored several miles off the coast of New Guinea one afternoon, Elmer Matson agreed to play ball on the main deck of our ship. All we were doing was throwing a ten-inch softball back and forth. Pretty soon, the inevitable happened: the ball got away from us and went over the side of the ship into the water. Even though we had about fifteen feet of freeboard (distance from the ship's deck down to the waterline), Elmer decided that since he was a good swimmer, he'd go after it. He wasted no time diving into the water and immediately swam right to the ball, which by now was slightly astern of us. Elmer turned around in the water and began to paddle back to the ship. At least, that's what he was trying to do. But with every stroke of his arms he got farther and farther away. We didn't know it at the time, but he was being pulled away by a six-knot current (about seven miles an hour). I wanted to send one of our two boats after him, but one boat was on the davit in a disabled condition and the other had been taken ashore on some business. Just then, someone threw Elmer a life ring. By continuing his strokes, he could forestall his drifting enough for the life ring to catch up with him. As he appeared smaller and smaller in the ocean, I wondered how and if we were going to save him! I thought that we might be seeing the last of Elmer Matson. Fortunately, within a few minutes, our boat returned to the ship; we sent it out immediately to rescue him. To this day when I see Elmer on one of his sojourns from Seattle, he continues to pale when I remind him of this event.

All in all, we spent a total of about nine months going back and forth between various islands of the Philippines such as Leyte, Samar, Cebu, Mindanao, Luzon, and Mindoro. We saw many other islands, too, as we passed by.

The rainy season in the Philippines is a time of mud in many places. The roads were either dusty or muddy, depending on the season. One day as I walked down one of these roads, I saw a man and his wife preparing their food over an open fire in their yard. Without hesitation, they offered to have me join them for fish heads and rice. With heartfelt thanks, I declined, but I surely felt compassion for these people who were willing to share their meager meal with me.

We also went to Saipan in the Marianas, where I walked along the shore at Marpi Point, the site of a great Japanese tragedy: many of the people on this island had hurled themselves off the cliffs in fear of the forthcoming U.S. invasion.

Guam and Tinian are also in this group of islands. Every morning we could see the B-29 long-range bombers take off from Tinian for their flight to Tokyo. Then in the afternoon, those planes that had survived the attack came straggling back. Some of them were quite disheveled, and I prayed that they would be able to land safely.

Shortly after the atomic bombs were dropped, the war in the Pacific ended, and we were in Tokyo Bay about two weeks later. It wasn't long before I was walking down the street in the Tokyo-Yokohama area, observing the absolute destruction of the cities. Where houses had once stood, only steel safes and fireplaces were left. Our fire bombs had done a devastating job. We also went to the northwest coast, docking at Aomori, where I was able to acquire a Japanese rifle to bring to Daddy. Another sojourn was offered to me at this time: a jeep ride up the slopes of Mount Fujiyama. How I wanted to go! However, it was a Sunday, and I had the opportunity to go to Mass; I dared not swap.

In December 1945 in a flurry of snow, we left Sasebo, Kyushu, Japan, for San Diego. After the long, uneventful trip, we finally arrived in the U.S. on January 6, 1946. We spent some time in San Diego and then moved the ship up to San Francisco.

Soon, I was granted a couple of weeks leave, so I took a train to Chicago, where I caught the Panama Limited to New Orleans.

On my return to California, we spent several weeks in San Francisco Bay, and then I was detached from the LST-712, which was being decommissioned. I was ordered to the LST-683 in Vallejo, California. This vessel was also in the process of being decommissioned. Around 1991 I saw a copy of a microfilm navy record that showed that I was transferred to the 683 to take over the command of that ship. That report is in error. I never was the Commanding Officer, only the Executive Officer, second in command. I participated in the activities necessary to prepare the ship for storage, which we called "putting the ship in mothballs."

Once when I was on a 24-hour tour of duty as Officer of the Deck while we were tied up to a buoy in the harbor, I had a strange experience. As was our prerogative while on this type of assignment, I turned

Vestigia

in at night with instructions to the men who were on duty to call me if any problems occurred. Sometime in the middle of the night, they did just that. They awakened me with the report that one of our men was trying to steal a boat. I had never heard of such a thing. I immediately asked what action they had taken. One of the duty officers replied to me, "I knocked him out." Sure enough, when I went out to the ship's gangway and looked over the side into our boat that was tied there, I beheld a sailor who was out cold, lying in the boat. On my instructions, the men aroused the culprit and brought him aboard. I learned that the unexpected is to be expected.

After only about one month aboard the LST-683, I was sent back to New Orleans to be separated from service. I couldn't get discharged because I was an Officer in the Reserves: I was given a Certificate of Satisfactory Service.

In the meantime, Albert had been released from prison by the advancing American forces. He was finally home again and quickly succeeded in putting back on the fifty or so pounds he had lost during his three marches across Poland. I couldn't begin to compare my experiences with his. How utterly miserable it must have been for him to be a prisoner of war: wearing the same clothes for eight and a half months, corralled into barns and locked up for the night, herded into boxcars that our own planes strafed, going for three days without water, and developing open sores caused by lice. He had it really rough! Such a test of his character, it was.

Now that I was out of the service, I had to concentrate on my future. It was my father's suggestion that I pursue a license with the Merchant Marine as a possible means of livelihood. With this in mind, I attended the Coast Guard upgrade school in New Orleans and became licensed as a Third Mate in the U.S. Merchant Marine. I was licensed to sail with this rank on vessels of any gross tonnage on any ocean. As time would tell, even though I renewed this license several years later, I never used it to go to sea.

All veterans were given the opportunity of attending school by the G.I. Bill of Rights. I therefore returned to Loyola, where I had been enrolled before the call to active duty in July of 1943.

In 1947 I met Marion Dueñas, my neighbor across the street. She was returning from Sunday Mass with her mother. Actually, I had been introduced to Marion by J.D. Early much earlier, when she was about 15 years of age, as she was passing in front of my house on Royal

Street. At that time she had been living in an upstairs apartment over Evola's Grocery on Governor Nicholls and Royal Street, a half block away.

Granny already was acquainted with Marion. She would sit on our front gallery and at times talk over the railing and across the street to Marion on her porch. Granny was my matchmaker. Marion had recently returned from New York, where she had graduated from Roosevelt Hospital as a Registered Nurse. She went to work at Oschner Foundation Hospital in Jefferson Parish and sometimes invited me to dances staged by the nurses.

I had known Marion's parents, Victor and Irma Dueñas, by sight but had never really met them. Irma worked in the Catholic Book Store, and Victor was an upholsterer of the highest quality. He was a hard-working man who, for seventeen years, did every kind of maintenance job at the Hotel Monteleone on Royal Street. I don't believe that he had any time off for holidays or vacations. Later his employment got better when he worked for an elite upholstering firm, but he still worked hard and received low pay. He kept his goal of retirement in sight: he wanted to buy some land across the lake and build a house on it. Irma did not share that desire. She preferred to remain in the city where her friends were. Nevertheless, she knew that the pending move was for their good, and she worked toward that end.

Hurricanes were scary things, and we had a few of them. Years ago we never had sophisticated data to track them and to broadcast progress as we have today, so I guess we never actually knew how poorly off we were. I got the message good one time when a hurricane struck in 1947. Marion and I walked around, exploring the damage after the storm. I had been taught by Daddy and Mother to be prepared during all storms with blessed candles, and when lightning would strike we were taught to say, "God bless us and save us."

My schedule of studies at Loyola was particularly challenging, not because of mathematics and physics, which held my primary interest, but because of German. I had selected German as the language to meet my degree requirement for a major in mathematics and a minor in physics. Mr. Victor Baker, a native of Vienna and former journalist there, was my professor. His ideas and mine did not coincide. Since he expected everyone who completed four semesters under him to speak the language, we had many exercises in German. The only course that I ever failed in school was this one,

Vestigia

the first semester German. Ironically, I had had a semester of German while I was attending Tulane in the navy program. However, when I was back at Loyola to continue my studies, my German credit was not accepted because it was too elementary. Consequently, I repeated first semester German only to experience failure. With a determined and exhaustive effort, I continued German at Loyola under Mr. Baker. It required a monumental effort. In fact, there was a time when I became so unnerved that I questioned my sanity. I prayed hard for the Lord to help me. It went like this:

We were given several sentences on page 78 of our text, *Deutsch Für Anfänger* (*German for the Beginner*), to translate for the next day. My method of remembering this assignment was to use my pencil to draw an arrow on that page pointing to the sentences. That night at home, when it came time to study German, I opened the book and looked around for an arrow. There was none. I looked and looked. I figured that someone had taken my book and erased the arrow, but that was not likely because I could see no impression on the page that I felt certain had the assignment. I coped with this dilemma by convincing myself that I had not actually made an arrow, but that I had meant to do so. I proceeded to translate those sentences that I really did recognize to be the proper assignment. Then I put my book away and worried myself to sleep.

Next day, back in class, I opened the book and was stunned—there was the arrow, right where it belonged. Was it the light that had tricked me? Was it the type of pencil? What was it? As the class progressed and it came time again for the day's assignment to be announced, I was ready. I took my pencil and firmly drew an arrow on page 96 to mark it for sure. This time I kept my book to myself, firmly in my grasp. Nobody was going to get their hands on it. Nervously, I took my book in hand when I got home and turned to the homework page. There was no arrow on it—and just to make matters worse, there was no arrow on page 78, either. Things really looked bad. Somehow, I managed to do my assignment and go to bed. I anticipated my arrival in class—what would I find this time?

Next day, the time came. I walked into class and sat down. Carefully, I opened the book—and there they were—both arrows were in their proper places, and I knew I must be nuts! I figured that from studying so hard I had driven myself crazy. Now it seemed to be time to see a doctor, but what kind of doctor? I made a decision. I would say a prayer to the Lord and then wait out the class for the 45 or so remaining minutes. If by that time I had not come up with a solution, I was going to deem myself sick and find medical help.

Once again, God showed that He heard me. By the time class ended, I had come up with the absolutely certain solution to my arrow problem: my German book had an error in its binding, and several chapters were erroneously duplicated. I would see the sections marked with arrows at school when I opened my book in one fashion and see no arrows at home when I opened it the other way. I immediately thanked God for restoring my sanity. I don't use arrows very much anymore.

Originally, I had been in a class of twenty-four students. Now when I had advanced to my fourth semester, I was the sole survivor. Others had either failed or dropped out. I, too, came close in this last semester, having received a conditional grade in the final exam—thus requiring a repeat test. I even went so far as to quit the course. This happened one day when Mr. Baker told me I was crazy. My immediate response was, "I don't take that from anybody!" I slammed my book closed. He interpreted my gestures as final, and I guess they were, because we both walked out of the classroom. Marion was the one who saved my hide. She convinced me that I should apologize to the professor for my impatience. When I did so, he accepted me back into his class, where I was again his only student. He explained to me then that he had often heard fellow professors speak to each other that way. That is why he used it as a colloquial expression. I then explained to him that a professor does not talk to his students in that manner. I studied and took my final exam again, and only by the skin of my teeth did I pass. Before this series of events, I had successfully completed my three necessary comprehensive mathematics exams.

Joe was a few years behind me in college. In my role as a Teacher's Assistant at Loyola, I was assigned the task of grading the students' papers, including Joe's. Ultimately, he outdistanced me when he gained his Master's Degree in Physics at St. Louis University. I felt a certain camaraderie with him in the field of science.

When I was a senior at Loyola, I got a part-time job across the river in Harvey with the National Geophysical Company—most boring. Actually, oil exploration is very interesting, especially for a geologist. Since I didn't have that expertise, I was given a more mundane assignment. When I graduated from Loyola, they wanted me to work full time

Vestigia

and spend some of my days on one of their boats exploring in the Gulf of Mexico. No, not for me!

Marion and I were engaged at Christmas of 1947. I heeded my mother's advice and agreed to delay marriage until I finished college, which would be later in 1948. I paid about $100 at Krower Jewelry store for her engagement ring, which was a fraction of a carat. I thought I was getting a bargain because Daddy used to work there—but I really didn't do so hot.

In August, I received a degree of Bachelor of Science with a major in Mathematics and a minor in Physics. Finally, seven years after I had started college, I was able to graduate. While some others went on to graduate school at LSU, I had had it! Enough was enough.

Chapter Five

Marriage

Marion and I were married in the St. Louis Cathedral on November 27, 1948, at ten o'clock Mass, I believe. Our wedding breakfast (reception) was hosted by Mr. and Mrs. Dueñas (about $90) at Arnaud's, a historic New Orleans restaurant. For our honeymoon, we went to Biloxi, Mississippi, and we also spent several days in Lacombe at the new house that Mr. Dueñas was building.

Marion quit Oschner and started working at Charity Hospital. After I had left my geophysical job, employment wasn't easy to find. At least I was able to get a job with the Archdiocese of New Orleans, collecting money for the pledges that had been made to the Youth Progress Program. I was paid $35 a week, which sufficed until I was able to join the U.S. Army Corps of Engineers at Prytania and the river in January of 1949. I worked as an estimator in the Contracts Estimate Section. Since my college degree was in Mathematics, I didn't have the necessary engineering degree to get a professional Civil Service classification. Instead, I had a Semi-Professional (SP) rate. I was an SP5 and later became an SP6, whereas I wanted to be a P1 or P2. We were living in an apartment at 813 Royal Street (owned by Aunt Aline, pronounced "Eileen," and Uncle Herbert—Daddy's brother). My means of transit was an aged International red panel truck that Mr. Arthur Jackson had asked me to keep running for him. Mr. Jackson didn't drive, and his wife was at a stage in life when she decided she no longer wanted to drive. She must have been in shock after just retiring from her role in the circus as the partner of the knife thrower; she had been the "target." I also understood that it might be helpful if I taught Mr. Jackson to drive. I took him out to City Park for a lesson behind the wheel. I never agreed to drive with him again after he put such fear in me at a fork in the road when he couldn't decide on which side of a tree he wanted to drive.

Numerous times we used the red panel truck to carry supplies and equipment to Poinciana, the Dueñas home across Lake Pontchartrain in

Lacombe. Papa and Mama welcomed the transportation, even though the seating was not very comfortable. It was more economical than taking the bus, and it provided door-to-door convenience. That vehicle wasn't without excitement, though; for example, at one point I had to replace a fuel pump when gasoline began to spurt out of the engine block. Periodically, I used a match stick to plug up a corroded hole in a freeze plug; I frequently replenished the water from the full bucket that I carried with me in the truck. The greatest thrill was provided one dark night while we were on the Maestri Bridge in the middle of Lake Pontchartrain on a cold trip to Poinciana with Papa, Mama, and the dog, Blackie. We were pushing 60 when suddenly the headlights went out and I was left to steer a straight course in the dark on this two-lane bridge. If not for the power of prayer, I would not be here to write this story. Intermittently the truck's power came on again. At a slower speed and with the aid of a flashlight beam, which Papa aimed at the center divider line, we were able to reach the other side of the lake. My diagnosis was right: we had a stuck voltage regulator. When I rapped it abruptly with a tool, it came back to life. That proves the old adage "If it doesn't work, kick it."

Mr. and Mrs. Dueñas helped us buy five acres of land in Lacombe. This plot was directly adjacent to their five-acre property. It provided assurance to them of isolation. Isolation is the real reason that you move out into open spaces such as Lacombe.

Once again, Daddy established a family band. This time it was with encouragement from Joe and me. One outsider, a Mr. Arrowsmith, played the violin while Joe played the trumpet, Marion played the clarinet, and I played the alto saxophone. Daddy, as usual, was on the piano. As always, our greatest admirer and ever-present audience was Mother. I thought that our music showed some potential. My favorite selection for this group was "Un Bel Di" from *Madame Butterfly* by Puccini. That was his real name, and that's what everybody called him. I admired the composer so much that I always thought of him by his full name: Giacomo Antonio Domenico Michele Secondo Maria Puccini. Because I remembered things like this, I guess it explains why I was also able to recall the value of pi to twenty-six decimal places.

My father's youngest brother, Rudolph, was a talented musician. This uncle had played professionally for many years with bands like Frankie Masters and the musical group that played on the *Fibber McGee and Molly* radio show. Also, he toured the country in his trailer

Vestigia

for the Conn Band Instruments Company of Elkhart, Indiana. In this capacity I saw him once at Werlein's Music Store on Canal and Chartres Streets. As a representative of Conn, he offered to play any selection on the clarinet or saxophone for the visitors to the store. I remember when he came to our house and played the mandolin. That was the first time I had ever heard that instrument. His selection, "The Holy City," was absolutely beautiful.

Years later, when Uncle Rudolph had limited his recitals and I could no longer hear him, I was so sad. By this time, I had finally grown to enjoy music. Evidently, Daddy must have conveyed to Uncle Rudolph my utmost appreciation for him, because one day Daddy informed me that Uncle Rudolph would be visiting from Chicago and would play clarinet for me. I was surprised and overjoyed to get this news. Uncle Rudolph, an absolute master of the clarinet and saxophone, who had previously stated that his future performances would be only for God, was now going to play for me! I was ecstatic. This certainly was not an opportune weekend for his visit. Marion and I were going to be across the lake with her parents, since we had many construction projects to do in Lacombe in connection with their future plans to move there.

However, I was able to use Mr. Jackson's red truck and return to New Orleans, forty-five miles each way, to hear this performance. Daddy sat at the piano. Then Uncle Rudolph picked up his clarinet and turned to me. "What would you like me to play?" he asked. For a moment I was speechless. After I made a quick recovery, I whipped out my book and showed him *La Sonnambula*. Immediately, with no preparation whatsoever, Daddy and he began to play this difficult number. Never during this performance was there any hesitation on the part of either one. It was spectacular! It was incredible! How fortunate I was to have recorded it on Daddy's Webcor wire recorder. Even though this unit had very poor frequency response, for whatever it was worth, I had it.

Some weeks thereafter, due to the scarcity of recording wire available for our use, this precious recording got completely wiped out. It was gone from the recorder, but it will never be gone from my mind. Rudolph Junior told me in later years that nearly all of his father's recordings were stolen when their home was robbed. Nevertheless, he was able to provide me with two wonderful tape recordings, which were made in the fifties. This, too, was an era of poor recording fidelity, but I took what I could get and was happy for it. I again settled into my clarinet regimen of *Hora Staccato*, by Dinicu and Heifetz, *Clarinet Polka*, *Schön Rosmarin*, *Flight of the Bumble Bee*, "Intermezzo" from *Cavalleria Rusticana* by Pietro Mascagni, and many other selections. My particular joy, however, was to play a medley of waltzes that I always concluded with a special dedication to my mother—"Let Me Call You Sweetheart." I learned these waltzes on the Mississippi River by listening to the band on the steamer *Capitol*. I had always admired the clarinetist on this ship. The nighttime trip that this paddle wheeler made on the river was a dance excursion that I made whenever possible. J.D. Early and I thought it was worth going just to listen to the music.

Because world events were changing dramatically now with the rise of Communism, I remembered the thoughts that I had had soon after the war, when I was still in Japan, I believed that Russia was up to no good. I had hoped that we would settle our differences with them before coming home; otherwise, we would have to go back on duty again. The comment made years ago by Schiller was most appropriate at this time: "Der Krieg ernährt den Krieg"—"War fosters war." Well, it was just a few years before my fears came true and the Cold War got started. Now I wanted to be sure that any future tour of duty would station me on land (the beach, as we called it), because I was tired of those underway watches aboard ship in the dark of night with the attendant responsibilities. In order to achieve this plan of mine, and also as a way of earning necessary money, I joined the Organized Reserves.

Marion did not work many weeks after we got married, and fortunately we had no urgent need for her ever to work again. We did, however, toy with the idea from time to time of having her work a little in order to maintain her credentials. She was a "Scrub Nurse," and she was the best in the business. When she scrubbed for an operation, the surgeon had a nurse by his side who knew the exact instruments he would use and when he would want them. Before we were married, I had the opportunity of witnessing her in action one night when there was an emergency exploratory operation for which she was needed. She was on call at the time, and I was visiting her at the hospital. The surgeon agreed to let me go into surgery and witness what turned out to be an appendectomy. His only requirement was that I touch nothing. And that's exactly what I did, even though the afflicted appendix, locked in the jaws of Kelly clamps, was passed around to each of the operating team for viewing. I stepped aside and looked at it but did not touch. Also, when someone dropped a whole tray of equipment onto the floor (thus contaminating it), I did not help to pick it up.

Even though I have developed very little tolerance for Mardi Gras, I do believe that there is a great bit of romanticism in the Carnival Season process. I don't know what the current practices are, but I remember how they were sixty years ago and how they were depicted in the romantic novel *Crescent Carnival* by Frances Parkinson Keyes. I cite this work as a reference for those who enjoy the elements of southern folklore.

When I was in college, I had the opportunity of going to the Hermes Ball. This was the grand festivity that took place after the carnival organization called the "Krewe of Hermes" had finished their parade through the streets of New Orleans. With the playing of "El Condor," a splendid American Indian pageant was staged at the beginning of the ball. After the pageant, there were the customary "callouts," which were followed by general dancing.

Each member of the Krewe of Hermes was in full mask and almost impossible to identify. Affixed to his wrist was a small card that carried the names of about 15 debutantes or close friends who were seated next to the dance floor in what was termed the callout section. When it was time for the first dance to begin, the krewe gathered in the middle of the floor, surrounded by ushers. Each usher then stood beside his assigned krewe member and proceeded into the callout section to locate the designated dance partners named sequentially on the individual lists of the krewe for dance number one. She was escorted to her partner out on the floor. When all was ready, the first dance began. When it was over, the krewe member reached into a small bag tied around his wrist and gave a token gift to his partner. At that time, she was then escorted back to her seat, and an usher located the next callout for the krewe member for dance number two. A young lady could have one or more callouts during the evening, but it was not uncommon for her to have only one.

After all callout dances were completed, there was general dancing for about a half hour. Those attendees who were sitting "in the rafters" could now come down to the floor and participate. After the general dancing, the festivities were concluded.

The culmination of Mardi Gras was celebrated by the staging of the two most prestigious balls—Rex and Comus. Each of these krewes occupied one side of the municipal auditorium separated in two by a huge curtain. At midnight, the curtain was drawn, the two kings met to drink a toast, and Mardi Gras was over—Lent began. It was extremely difficult to procure tickets for this grandest of all the balls, but one year Mama Dueñas did the impossible: she got tickets for Marion and me.

While we were expecting our first child, I was prepared to drive Marion to Touro Infirmary for her delivery and was ready to use the red truck, even with its offending exhaust fumes. However, one of my friends, Malcolm Tuohy, had offered to drive across town from the Carrollton area where he lived to our apartment on Kerlerec Street. Since I couldn't be sure how much time Marion would need to get to the hospital, I always kept the truck ready to run. Fortunately, it was not needed for this trip.

On November 11, 1949, in the late afternoon, about 5:15, Francis Junior was born at Touro Infirmary after a hard day of labor for Marion. I gave her a dozen yellow roses; they were her favorite flower. On special occasions I gave her a single long-stem yellow rose, but for this very special occasion, I broke the precedent and gave her a dozen. Even from his very early days, Francis was an active, restless child who exhibited brilliance. When he was nine months old, Marion and I took him with us to Norfolk, Virginia, for my annual active duty navy training. We made the trip with a former Loyola classmate, John Strate, and his wife, Eloise, in the new Oldsmobile 88 that belonged to John's brother, Zack. On this trip I learned what a risky driver John was when he sometimes cruised at speeds in the nineties. After the trip was over, Zack had to get a new engine for his car. I supposed that the high-speed driving had wiped out the engine, but I was told that it really hadn't—though I'm not sure I believed him. Incidentally, Zack was rather successful in the construction business. It was he who erected the huge motel complex on the site of the former Pelican Stadium at Tulane and Carrollton Avenues. This stadium held many memories for me because my father would take us there to baseball games. It was there also that I met my boyhood baseball idol, Mel Ott, when he came for an exhibition game. Later, he was elected to the Hall of Fame.

I remember living on Kerlerec Street in New Orleans when we didn't have an operable washing machine. Clothes were hung out to dry, and when thunderstorms occurred, we rushed to take them in. I came home from work one afternoon and washed twenty-two diapers by hand. In those days, I don't remember any such thing as a disposable diaper.

Chapter Six

Another War

*I*n September 1950, I was recalled to active duty in the navy because of the Korean War. Once again, the navy decided that it needed amphibious sailors and therefore tended to disregard the specific training that I had been undergoing in the active reserve. My orders were to report to San Diego, California, and after refresher training I was to go to Bremerton, Washington, to become part of the crew of the LST-1101. Mother and Mrs. Dueñas agreed to share the care of Francis so that Marion could travel by train with me to San Diego. John Strate had been called to duty about two weeks before me, so he and Eloise preceded us to San Diego with the agreement that they would rent an apartment for the four of us. When Marion and I got to San Diego, John had already gone to his duty assignment in Korea. I finally saw John months later when I bumped into him in Korea. Now, Marion and I lived with Eloise on Quince Street in San Diego for a couple of weeks during my training, and then Eloise left for New Orleans. When it was time for us to go to Bremerton, we took a train and then were successful in finding a reasonably priced motel in the general proximity of the naval shipyard where my future ship, the LST-1101, was being refurbished. Dan Stokes and his wife and child were staying just up the hill from us. Dan came from Mansfield, Louisiana, and had been with me at V-12 school in New Orleans. He had come to Bremerton because he was assigned to another LST in this same area. This was an opportune friendship for us then, because Dan had an automobile and thus provided frequent rides. Marion was expecting Linda at the time, and therefore we were very grateful for the transportation. It was November 1950 now, and it was so rainy in Bremerton across Puget Sound from Seattle that I made note of the fact that in six weeks, there were only two days in which we didn't see rain.

While we were in the Seattle area, we visited Elmer Matson and his wife, Polly. We drove with them up to Vancouver, Canada, and got caught in the worst fog that I have ever seen. We could see absolutely

69

nothing. As a result, we had to park the car immediately, wherever that happened to be, and we remained in that spot for hours. It was an experience that I would not want to go through again.

The following excerpt, which is pertinent to this era, is taken from the introduction to a book, *Our Guide*, which I wrote in 1986:

> It is obvious to me now that the Lord knew from the very beginning that I would need the best of help in order to guide me; He never hesitated to provide. In times of greatest need, I could always be sure that God would hear my prayers. A vivid example was in 1950 in Bremerton, Washington, during the Korean War (which had been the reason for my recall to naval service). I was assigned to a ship that was still in "moth balls" and was being re-activated for service. It was hardly habitable; therefore, portions of the crew, including myself, were permitted to live ashore. Realizing that I might never come back from the war alive, I seized the opportunity to have my wife, Marion, travel from New Orleans with me on this assignment to share a few weeks together. Our only child was left at home in the care of our parents, and Marion was in the latter stages of pregnancy with our second child. The weather was dismal, rainy, and depressing; our quarters were in a simple motel along the road outside of town. In our last few days before I was sent with this ship overseas, while it was still being renovated, I left Marion one Sunday morning and obtained a ride with someone to the Navy base for a day of duty as Officer of the Deck. I told Marion that if she wanted to go to church, she would have to hitchhike, for we had no car. That she did, willingly, even with her physical discomfort. As a means of remaining together spiritually, we had swapped rosaries—my wooden beads had become hers, and her large crystal beads with the ornate silver crucifix had become mine. Having boarded the ship to begin my duty, I dismissed the two enlisted men who were on watch at the gangway; I figured it was a good time for them to go below for coffee. Soon thereafter, I entered the officer's restroom and closed the door. Immediately, I noticed that the knob and shaft were missing and the door was hopelessly locked. Realizing that no one else was on this entire deck, I knew that shouting or noise-making would

be fruitless; prayer alone would free me. Thus, I spoke briefly but confidently in prayer to Our Lady: "Dear Blessed Mother, if you want me to remain locked in this room, I will accept your will and wait until tomorrow when many people come aboard. Then, surely, I will be found; or, Blessed Mother, if you see fit, please let me out, so that I may go about my duties." I said one Hail Mary. Then, noticing only barren bulkheads, devoid of any implements, I reached into my pocket and found Marion's rosary. The ornate crucifix was the exact size to fit diagonally into the door latch; I turned it easily and opened the door.

Since our galley facilities were not functioning on the LST at this time, we took a short trip down the dock each day at noon to the USS *Indiana*. I couldn't imagine when I was a boy that the day would come when I'd eat lunch every day on a battleship.

When our ship was commissioned, Marion left from the Seattle-Tacoma airport for New Orleans, and the ship sailed out of the Straits down the coast to San Diego as our shakedown cruise (that was how a ship was tested). Upon arrival in San Diego, I began a futile search for an apartment so that Marion might come out to California with little Francis to join me. I was resolved to find a place for us to stay. But no matter how hard I tried, there was no place to be found. Obviously, it was time for the Lord to step in. Near Christmas, as I was standing (in uniform, of course) at a bus stop, a lady approached me asking if I would be with my family at Christmas. When I replied that it would not be possible since I had no place for my wife and child, she mentioned that her landlady, Mrs. West, had an extra room in her house and that perhaps she would rent it out. I pursued that possibility with haste. When the deal was cast in brass, I called Marion and she flew with Francis to Lindbergh Field in San Diego where I met them.

As it turned out, this small place in which we were now living was a major challenge for the three of us, because Francis was exceptionally precocious and Mrs. West was a sedate, older lady who lived alone and kept everything in its precise place.

We had made friends with a navy wife who was living in San Diego while her husband was at sea on a destroyer. I don't recall her first name; we used to call her "Mac," since her last name was MacMurphy.

Marion and I were unable to keep Francis corralled in our limited space. Still searching and praying, we were again blessed through our friend, Mac, to find a garage apartment that was very, very minimal, but for us it was absolutely great. It was there that we stayed until late January or early February, when my ship had to sail to the Long Beach shipyard. Once again, Marion flew home to New Orleans, where she and Francis were to stay until my return from Korea.

At the Long Beach shipyard, we made our final overseas preparations. Gertrude happened to be stationed at Boyle Heights in Los Angeles at the time, and when I phoned her to say goodbye before going overseas, she said, "Can't I come see you?" Wow! How does a Sister of Charity get into and around the shipyard in a regular habit with a huge cornet on her head? "Sure," I answered; she was welcome to do so. I was so surprised and happy the next day to see two automobiles drive up, loaded with Sisters of Charity. Manuel, their driver, whom I had already met, was there, and in one of the cars was a Sister Catherine with the crooked finger (as I designated her). This Sister at some later time became the Visitatrix (the title given to a provincial). I gave them a grand tour of the ship and felt that they had given me a royal sendoff for my new tour of duty overseas. To the tune of "Anchors Aweigh" on the P.A. system, we pulled out of the harbor. That was indeed a sad moment for me, because I knew that Marion would be delivering our second child soon, whereas I was going on to some unknown future in a type of ship and in an environment that I was only too familiar with. I felt the pain down to my toes.

When I was on the LST-1101, some members of the crew asked me to be their "chaplain." I thought the request to be rather humorous, so I gave it no further attention. Repeated requests came, and finally I received a written petition signed by many members of the crew. Now, just as in previous similar situations, I knew that I would do my best to provide church services for the crew, but I was not inclined to assume the title of Chaplain. I did, however, apply my efforts in this regard for the duration of my assignment on this ship.

We stopped at Pearl Harbor in Hawaii and then moved on across the ocean. I was quite proficient at Morse code from early instruction that Daddy had given me, thus I was able to copy radio code fairly well and read the inter-ship blinking light signals just as well as our signalmen. On duty as the Officer of the Deck one day, I made it my business to read the incoming light signal at the same time that the signalman

Vestigia

was getting it. This was a seldom-received type of transmission called an "E Message." Personal messages (telegrams), which for tactical purposes are the lowest priority, carry this classification. I was shocked to see that this message was for me! It read, "For Lieutenant Francis Levy 384517, Granny died, Linda was born."

Daddy had sent me this message, and as we had pre-arranged, he presented two dozen yellow roses to Marion. It was my plan to give Marion an added dozen roses each time a child was born. It didn't take me long to realize that this plan had to be scrapped.

While at sea, if conditions permitted, I held a church service aboard ship on Sundays for all who wished to attend. My format was to read the Gospel and follow with the Rosary. On one of those Sundays, I managed to get into a repetitive sequence during the Rosary where I couldn't get past one of the phrases of the Apostles' Creed. I, their leader, fumbled with the words of this prayer, which I had said countless times. That was a profound lesson in humility.

For the next several months, we sailed back and forth between Japan and Korea to such places as Inchon, Pusan, and Cheju Do. Besides ferrying troops and equipment to the battle zone, we were stationed off the western coast of Korea to await possible necessary evacuation of our troops in case of a rout by the enemy. Fortunately, that didn't happen, but the troops knew that we were there just in case.

The navy doesn't look very kindly on someone going AWOL (absent without leave). During the Korean War, we had one of these situations, and our captain set up a three-officer court martial board to try the case. Since I was the senior officer of this group, I ran the entire proceedings. Even though I never wanted to follow my father's legal profession, I now found myself up to my ears in a legal trial about which I knew very little. I was the president of a court that had to conform to the Uniform Code of Military Justice. The irony of it all was the fact that our captain, Samuel G. Blalock, was an attorney in civilian life, and unless there was some rule prohibiting it, I thought that he should have handled the case. I studied hard so that we would render justice to this sailor who was before our court. In a few days, we completed the proceedings and found the man guilty. He was demoted, fined, and sentenced to time in the brig. When our court recordings were sent to the office of the Judge Advocate, they were returned to us with various notations of procedural errors, but the case was approved as conducted. That was the end of my career as a judge.

When a ship goes into port, the one thing on everybody's mind is "liberty." When sailors are ashore and get into trouble during liberty, they are usually escorted by the Shore Patrol back to their ship, where justice is administered. In Japan one time, I was assigned as the senior officer of a Shore Patrol contingent. This was completely different from anything I had ever done. My greatest concern at that time was the possibility of some entanglement between U.S. sailors and the Japanese police. Fortunately, we didn't run into much trouble, and no problem ever arose with the Japanese. I was greatly relieved to have that assignment behind me. That was the end of my career as a police lieutenant.

Another time while we were overseas, a member of our crew had gotten involved in a fracas while ashore, resulting in a pair of broken glasses for one of the civilians. I was sent ashore to represent the navy and render an on-the-scene judgment. Quickly, it was decided to have the sailor pay for the replacement of the broken glasses, and further turmoil was avoided. That was the end of my career as an arbitrator.

The excessive drinking that takes place ashore sometimes results in drunken sailors coming back aboard ship. In cases where they are not drunk, they are often "under the influence." This happened one time, and there was noticeable unrest in the crew's quarters. One of our cooks, so I was told, was going to come up to the officer's galley and get a knife to take below in order to settle a score. This cook, a Filipino who always worked in our galley, was a quiet, well-behaved man who never caused any trouble. I didn't know what to expect, and I may have been the only officer on board at the time. I decided to lay in wait in the passageway where this man would have to pass in order to get back into the crew's quarters. Sure enough, in due time I saw my suspect come into sight. His facial expression showed that he was under the influence of some toxic substance, but his hands were empty. However, I felt certain that he had a knife because of the report that I had received. After a very earnest silent prayer, I ordered him to give me the knife. He pulled up his jumper and there, hidden, tucked into the waist of his pants, was a long bread knife. He reached down, pulled it out and gave it to me peacefully. Whew! Thank you, Lord. That was the end of my career as a drug enforcement officer.

There was a time of insurrection in the Prisoner of War (POW) camps that the U.S. had in Korea. When the Marines were called upon to quell the riots, our ship was one of those sent to one of these disturbances. We loaded up at the designated area and proceeded to the site of the riot. On the tank deck, our contingent of armed Marines with their engines running stormed out through the bow doors onto the beach and into the hostile prison. The technique that was used to quiet these situations was swift and effective.

Soon thereafter, we left Yokosuka, Japan, on our thirty-day trek home across the Pacific to San Diego. Fortunately, the trip was uneventful. (In the Addendum to this book there is a brief history of the LST-1101.) Because it was impossible to get a train or a plane, I took a bus home to New Orleans. I was dog tired when I arrived and greeted Marion and my new nine-month-old daughter, Linda, for the first time.

During the Korean conflict, I resolved to save enough money to buy a car when I got home. We did so according to plan; it was a new 1951 Chevrolet, two-door, blue Styleline De Luxe. We got it from the Wheeling Frenchman for about $1,800, which we financed through the Associates Discount Corporation for about $91.28 per month. I remember procuring automobile insurance through my sister Mary when she was working for an insurance company. On numerous occasions, she provided me with "binders." These interim commitments assured me of continuous insurance coverage.

When my two weeks leave was ending, we drove with Francis Jr. and Linda to San Diego. It was quite a trip, and I was very thankful that Marion was a nurse, because Francis got the mumps when we were near San Antonio. We continued our journey, but with the expected difficulties.

I had made plans with Al Villere, a former classmate of mine, to find an apartment for us in San Diego. Al was now married and living in San Diego on Narragansett Hill. I had left $100 with him for a down payment on the apartment, and therefore, I was sure it would be ready. Well, it wasn't. Al tried hard, but he wasn't successful in finding housing. He and Mary Katherine invited us to stay with them, mumps and all. We moved in with them until we were able to locate a place. Even though I had to spend my days aboard ship, we managed to find time to search the area. We were thankful to discover a whole floor of a house at 3966 Falcon Street in San Diego in an area called North Park for which we paid $100 per month. That was very steep.

I taught Marion to drive by using the hills of San Diego as our training grounds. Our Chevrolet had manual transmission, and at this time, shifting was done by a lever on the steering column. She did extremely well and soon learned to handle any hill, even though I frequently made her stop right in the middle of our ascent and then proceed upward with the necessary progressive shifting. Soon thereafter, she got her driver's license. One day in North Park, when she was stopped by a policeman because she had missed a stop sign, she was able to elicit sympathy from the officer and evade the ticket.

After we had lived for a while in San Diego, we moved to a Quonset hut in National City, which gave us cheaper rent since it was sponsored by the navy. Then, when the ship moved to Long Beach, we also moved our living quarters to another Quonset hut in San Pedro. It was in this location that I was awakened early one morning when a big earthquake rattled us. This was the quake that destroyed the prison in the city of Tehachapi. At four in the morning, I was barely able to stand amid the tremor. I believe that a Quonset hut is the safest structure in which to experience an earthquake, because it is so resilient.

Mr. and Mrs. Dueñas visited us in this location and stayed for a couple of weeks until I was released from duty in September, two years after my recall to service.

All of us then drove up to San Francisco to see Muriel at the Roman Catholic Orphanage (RCO). This was a venerable, old orphanage, just the type of home—although considerably larger—that the Daughters of Charity used to have all over the country. At this time, Marion was expecting our third child, Steve, and when we were ready to leave San Francisco, the doctor didn't deem it safe for her to journey with us by car to New Orleans. Thus, Marion flew to New Orleans with Linda while Mr. and Mrs. Dueñas went with Francis and me by car. We took several days to make the trip through King's Canyon National Park and other sites like the Grand Canyon.

Mama got very sick on our descent from high altitude, and only after we got back to sea level did she recover. I was surprised when we were going through the Painted Desert that Papa didn't think it to be very colorful. Later that evening, when it was dark, I found out the reason. I happened to be driving into the driveway of our motel, and I asked Papa to look out the window and help guide me. When he had difficulty seeing the ramp, I learned that he still had his sun glasses on. In fact, he had had sunglasses on all day and, obviously, he had missed the colorful beauty of the Painted Desert.

Back in New Orleans, we settled into the downstairs apartment in Daddy and Mother's house at 1123 Royal Street. While I was in Korea,

Marion had moved there with Francis and Linda because it was better for them to be near my parents rather than to be alone at 813 Royal Street where I had left them. This new apartment consisted of a bedroom, living room, kitchen, and bath. Before it was modified, besides having a bath, this area was essentially two large rooms: my father's workshop and the adjoining "washroom" that had been used by a Chinese laundry. Y Louie now had his laundry one block up the street.

I remember, in preceding years, helping my father renovate the washroom and helping to tear down the plaster in the "big room," which was 17½ x 45 feet. I know that the "big room" was also a part of the old laundry, but I don't remember it that way. What I remember very vividly is our relentless fight with termites in the downstairs flooring. Twice we were invaded by termites at 1123 Royal Street, and each time, they totally destroyed about 1200 square feet of flooring and even worked their way into the walls. Fortunately, the walls were double brick, so the termites could damage only the trim. The final solution to our problem was the laying of asphalt tile on top of concrete. Since there is no such thing as a concrete termite, we finally won the battle. The brick walls, however, tended to be a bit fragile due to their age. This house had been built in 1831, and the mortar of that day certainly wasn't the best. It had lasted over a hundred years, though, so what could one expect? I took it upon myself to repair these walls periodically by "pointing the bricks" (putting in new mortar to replace that which had crumbled out). I enjoyed doing repair work and took advantage of the many things that I had learned from my father.

I felt that our family had achieved significant recognition when my brother, Louis, won the annual Jackson Day Race one year in New Orleans. No one could have been more surprised than I as I met him at the finish line in Pirate's Alley. My joy was unbounded. It would be fascinating to review the events of history surrounding this race, but a synopsis might suffice. The Battle of New Orleans is a significant event in U.S. history; one of its most interesting aspects is that it took place after the War of 1812 was over. This battle at Chalmette actually took place in 1815, weeks after the Treaty of Ghent was signed in Europe. Major General Andrew Jackson, "Old Hickory," later to become our seventh president, commanded our forces, which were composed of units of the U.S. Army, former Haitian slaves, "long rifle" frontiersmen from Kentucky and Tennessee, and some outlaw pirates, including Jean and Pierre Lafitte. These men—4000 in number—faced more than twice that many in opposition under the British General Edward Pakenham. Jackson was victorious in this battle, and New Orleans was saved. To commemorate the joining of the forces that united under Jackson to defend the city, the annual Jackson Day race is staged.

This native son of South Carolina, who gained prominence in Tennessee and later as president of the United States, is memorialized in an equestrian statue, the centerpiece of Jackson Square, in view of the spires of the St. Louis Cathedral. When I was a boy, I remember the outrage of the populace when Andrew's head was toppled by exuberant youths. For days we had a headless horseman as our hero until patriotism finally won over and someone returned the missing head.

In later years, Louis continued his success as a distance runner, and when he received his master's degree in history, he became my "personal expert" in this field. I was able to phone him when I needed to resolve my historical questions.

Chapter Seven

Joining Industry

Once again, just as was the case after World War II, all veterans of military service were granted the G.I. Bill of Rights, whereby they received free schooling, rights to retention of their jobs, assistance in buying a home, and I think we got a cash bonus again. Pursuant to this law, I returned to the U.S. Army Engineers to reclaim my job. Now, I was told that my job had been abolished, and since they were obliged to re-hire me, they would place me in the Soils Lab, where they did a physical analysis of soil samples from areas throughout the South. After fooling around with core samples, baking and weighing and rolling wet mud to study plasticity, I became convinced that this wasn't for me. The compelling factor in this decision was the plight of a fellow worker who was quite capable and set in this position until I had come on the scene. Because this man was not a veteran, I was going to have to bump him. I couldn't do that, so I quit. Daddy came to my aid at that time by introducing me to a young man, Norvin Pellerin, the son of a client, Willis Pellerin, who sold laundry machinery. Norvin had recently graduated from Tulane as a mechanical engineer, and his father set him up in business with the idea that he would manufacture industrial laundry machinery. Another plan that was in mind was the production of bombs for the military. Although the bomb plan didn't materialize, the laundry machinery aspect did.

I was able to get a job at $400 a month for a 44-hour week (half a day on Saturday) because I answered Norvin's query about developing a special system for him. He wanted to devise an automatic injection system for all of the laundry supplies that are put into a commercial washing machine during its cycles. I told him that I could invent an injection system for all of the chemicals that were used merely by controlling the pH (hydrogen ion content) of the wash water. I said that I would achieve this by constantly measuring the electrical conductivity of the water and using the amount of this conductivity to control the injection process. This job was very interesting, and I enjoyed it immensely. I worked on the injection system and many other tasks that included electrical design and testing of industrial washers and extractors that were custom designed for many places throughout the world. I also worked with a variety of electrical specifications. When inspecting units for shipment, I was certified to perform the required dielectric withstanding voltage test for Canadian Standards (CS) labeling. This is a certification like the U.S. Underwriter's "UL" label.

I worked for three years with the Pellerin Milnor Corporation. (The word Milnor was a combination of Norvin's mother's name, Mildred, and Norvin's own name.) In order to keep up with my job, I spent many nights studying electricity and electrical components. Often, Daddy was with me at this time. Due to the environment, there was variability in the conductivity of the wash solutions, and I was not able to produce an automatic injection system that could be manufactured and marketed for a profit. The two things that were financially insurmountable were the fluctuations caused by temperature and the basic chemical content of the supply water. However, we did succeed in getting a patent. This patent (Control System—U.S. Patent Number 2,874,714) was credited to Norvin and me and properly assigned to Norvin, because he had financed the whole study. We were granted a patent for other work, also, but I never did actually see the paper.

On November 14, 1952, Stephen Victor was born. For the first two years of his life, Steve was sick. As early as two weeks of age, he presented us with a major emergency. Marion called me at work to say that he was "projectile vomiting." I had never heard of that phenomenon, but I soon learned what it meant: anything that went into Steve's mouth came right back out like a projectile out of a cannon. His system was refusing to accept food because there was a blockage somewhere. Instinctively, through her training, Marion spotted this situation as being of major importance. I hastened home, and we rushed Steve to the hospital, where the doctor was waiting to do emergency surgery. Dr. Billy Roy's opinion was right—Steve had a strangulated hernia that would have become gangrenous in another twenty-four hours. The former Loyola pole-vaulter, Billy Roy, had saved Steve's life. Corrective surgery was done again at a later age. Then, for a long period of time, Steve suffered from colds, earaches, and what have you.

I became interested in a new house in Metairie and made a $300 down payment to hold it. When I realized that the financing was actually over my head, I was able to wiggle out of that deal. In due time, we bought a new brick veneer home in Kenner, Louisiana, near the airport for $11,000 by paying notes of $77 per month. It was small but adequate except for the drainage, which backed up sometimes during rainstorms. We loved our home and made the most of it by adding things here and there. I assembled and installed solid-pipe clotheslines in the backyard, and Papa gave us a reel-type lawn mower to meet our needs.

We had pleasant neighbors, and all went well for the most part. One day, Francis came in the kitchen door, returning from play around the corner. He was all beaten up. After he explained to me what had happened, I told him to go right out the front door to deal with that boy who had beaten him. Pretty soon, one of the parents showed up at our door and complained to me. Fortunately, we settled the problem peacefully. I told Francis that he must never pick a fight, but surely whenever someone picks on him, he must defend himself—except if it is a girl.

"Don't hit a girl. If a girl ever hits you, run away," I told him.

Well, the next day, in walked Francis again, all beaten up.

"What happened now?" I asked.

"A girl hit me," he replied.

"Didn't I tell you to run away if a girl wants to hit you?"

"Yeah, Daddy, but I couldn't; she was sitting on me."

"Well, son," I said, "we're going to make a new rule: anytime a girl is sitting on you, you can hit her."

In the latter months of 1954 I had a spontaneous pneumothorax and chose our pediatrician to treat me because I trusted him. This lung collapse was diagnosed as being congenital. With the prayers of my family and all of the Daughters of Charity, I soon recovered. After much contemplation during this period of inactivity, I decided that I wasn't going to make it financially in my present job, and a change was needed. Liking my job was one thing, but not receiving adequate pay was another. I contacted IBM through some local recruiters, and they financed a weekend trip for me to Poughkeepsie, New York. It seemed that I had impressed all of the job interviewers there to the degree that it was only a matter of time before I would receive a job offer in the mail. No such luck. There was no explanation given in subsequent correspondence for this action. I believe the refusal was due to my Jewish name.

I continued my job search through the newspapers. California carried many ads for people to work in aerospace. I answered one such ad that Lockheed had for its Palmdale, California, facility. Without further ado, I was hired by mail, sight unseen. They gave me $420 per month for a forty-hour week and provided full company benefits (a new world for me). Also, we were to be paid $35 a day for travel and would be provided with motel expenses for one month on arrival in Burbank, California, where I was to report. We traded in our old car and bought a new 1955 Chevrolet four-door, V8 sedan and were fortunate enough to be able to sell our house immediately for $1,500 cash and assumption of mortgage. Now we were ready to leave Louisiana for good; we loaded the car and hit the road.

Our trip to California was long and hot. It was 109 degrees when we pulled into Burbank, and we were full of the orange juice that we had continually stopped for on the road. Marion had the children lie down on the tile floor of the motel bathroom to keep cool.

Now we were in California with our new car, with only 3000 or so miles on the odometer. Already, though, it had a pair of worn-out tires on the front end. Soon, I realized the cause of this phenomenon: while Marion was driving through Louisiana on a two-lane road in a heavy rainstorm, I thought she couldn't see all of the road and I shouted to her that she was going to go off the right side of the road. When she swerved to avoid this apparent calamity, the car spun completely around. With visibility badly impaired, I opened my door and jumped out to run around to the other side in order to switch drivers. As I opened the door, Marion's purse fell out onto the road. I stooped over and gathered the contents that had spilled out, then raced around to the driver's side and got in while Marion went over to the other side. How stupid I was! I later realized that pulling such antics in the rain on a two-lane highway with such low visibility was very foolish. Having spun around, we were now going in the wrong direction. It took a while to locate an opportunity to turn. I didn't know it at the time, but this violent maneuver put our front end so far out of line that we ruined our tires very soon.

I had two weeks of training in Burbank, and then, as planned, I was transferred to Palmdale as an Instrumentation Engineer for the airplanes that were being tested there. We rented a house at 1368 East Avenue R2 in Palmdale. There was no air conditioning, but we were comfortable enough with a swamp cooler that was already on the roof. Marion seemed to have lost some of her vibrancy in our new location. Surely, she had good cause for a letdown with the trauma of events. She felt that her gloom was caused by the absence of music, so I bought her a new Voice of Music (VM) high-fidelity record player. She was in her glory! I enjoyed it just as much. I worked a lot of overtime doing a job that I enjoyed. The weather was clear every day, but the winds were atrocious. In the winter it got cold, as low as 18 degrees, and in the summer it got hot, as high as 110 degrees—but the sky was always clear.

When it was time for our redhead, Gail, to be born, Mama came to Palmdale to help us; what a blessing that was! Also, we enjoyed her company very much. As Gail grew older, she was my pride and joy. There was no prettier and no sweeter smiling baby in all the world. Here and in later times I would put Gail into the stroller and push her around the block. I called her "Carrot," and I showed her off to everybody. I could never tell when Gail was sick, because she was always smiling. I remember even when she had a fever of 103 she smiled.

We made occasional trips over the mountains to San Gabriel to visit Gertrude, who had by then moved to Maryvale. This was the new orphanage for the Sisters of Charity, replacing the one that they previously had in Boyle Heights. It was always a most enjoyable trip when we went to Maryvale. All of the Sisters were in love with our children, and we spent most of our time with Sister Frances, Sister Elizabeth, and Gertrude. The manner in which Gertrude handled the emotional problems of those who were in her charge was absolutely remarkable. She had a special routine that she used to quiet them down when they returned to the orphanage after having spent a weekend of turmoil with their family.

Francis started school, and Marion was kept very busy in the house with Linda, Steve, and Gail. Linda was a good baby, and as she grew older, she was a great help to her mother. Marion gave her the nickname "Winge." There were sufficient playmates in the area for the children. Steve especially enjoyed playing in our small backyard with one of the boys who lived close by. Whenever we looked out of the window for Steve, there he was with the other little towhead neighbor, playing.

One day, Steve got a bright idea. He told his mother that he was going to run away. This could have been a problem, because although we were in a housing tract, from the backyard outward there was nothing between us and the mountains. Marion maintained her calm at Steve's announcement. She told him, "Be sure that you take a stick with you."

"A tick?" he replied. "Why a tick?"

Marion answered, "To kill the snakes."

"Nakes?" questioned Steve.

Immediately he dropped the whole plan.

On another occasion, Steve suffered a mishap while supposedly taking a nap. He used the bed as a trampoline that failed to catch his fall. It was Marion's expertise again that provided the diagnosis of Steve's condition, a broken clavicle.

At Palmdale I worked for Joe Csongradi, a pleasant, knowledgeable engineer. For fifteen months we tested airplanes. Specifically, I worked on the T2V, a navy trainer plane that actually was a further development of the Air Force T33 trainer. I also worked on the F104B, which was a two-seat version of the red-hot F104 fighter plane. Those were very, very exciting days that I spent on the flight line. Although my job called for me to fly with my test equipment whenever my plane was being tested, there was no room on these planes for an engineer. Also, during training in Burbank, they had decided not to put me in the test chamber to experience explosive decompression because of my previous history of a spontaneous pneumothorax. Thus I was not certified for these kinds of flights.

Flight test for Lockheed at Palmdale involved the technology of the time. We had the best equipment available as well as a shop ready at our beck and call to manufacture the many special devices, custom made to our requirements. The prototype planes assigned to the test programs were stripped of any non-essential equipment in order to provide room for this specially designed instrumentation, which was necessary to evaluate flight worthiness. For any given plane, it required several weeks and numerous flights to complete the test series. The greatest capability of the program, however, lay in the ability of the test pilots. These were a remarkable group of men whom we got to know and work with on a daily basis. Theirs was a dangerous job, for they were taking new designs through maximum-stress maneuvers never before attempted by these planes.

Strain gauges were placed at various locations on the control surfaces of a plane to measure the forces that were applied to that surface. Air speed, stall speed, ground speed, and other parameters were measured to ascertain the worthiness of the aircraft. One special test that had to be conducted in one of my programs was a groundspeed test where the plane was to be accelerated to maximum ground speed but was not allowed to take off. At peak speed, the brakes were to be forcefully applied. This maximum breaking force was to bring the plane to a screeching stop. Then, with a brief turnaround, the same routine was to be repeated in the reverse direction. For this test, special instrumentation was installed on the aircraft and the necessary calibrations were made. The last operation to be performed prior to test was the flipping of the master instrumentation switch to begin recording data; that was my final contribution to the proceedings.

The test pilot did just as he was supposed to do, and all of the flight crew did, as well. The plane went back and forth at high speed on the ground and repeatedly came to a quick stop each time that the pilot applied the brakes. It was obvious that the ultimate pressures had been applied, for the brakes were sizzling with the heat. Now that the test was concluded, the pilot brought the plane back to our initial starting area, jumped out of the cockpit, and exclaimed how well the operation had gone and let us know that he knew for sure he had accumulated excellent data. Everybody was elated and smiling, except one man, the instrumentation engineer—me. Just moments before, I had come to the realization that this test was an absolute flop. I had failed to flip on the instrumentation switch!

The responsibility and challenge that is presented to a test pilot is very great. These men are generally the most experienced and capable of all the men who fly. Aircraft companies risk a lot of money on their new designs, and the flight test programs for these new aircraft are quite expensive. It is fascinating to work in this environment and learn from the cream of the crop. When my job called for me to make trips between Burbank and Palmdale, this would sometimes be accomplished by using our own company's shuttle flights, which took the shortest route over the mountains. Often, we would have test pilots at the controls for these flights. One of our planes at the time was an old reliable DC3. I remember once that I was the lone passenger on one of these flights. Another memorable occasion on a smaller aircraft was a flight at dusk, skimming over the treetops on the mountain as I sat next to the test pilot.

After working for Lockheed for fifteen months without a promotion, I pursued greener pastures. This time it was in Pomona, California, with General Dynamics. Here was a new field to explore—missiles! I began work on December 15, 1956. My first assignment was to produce a correlation drawing for the navy's Tartar missile. By studying the missile and working with the design groups who were responsible for each of the missile segments, I coordinated the information and directed the drafting group in the production of a composite drawing. This task provided good orientation for me in this new enterprise.

We purchased a newly constructed four-bedroom home in La Verne, California. It was about $16,000 and required payments of about $137 per month. It wasn't easy to meet our financial needs, but God always provided. On September 6, 1957, Dan was born. Fortunately, he was a healthy child and didn't present any special medical challenge. Marion's efficiency made our household run very smoothly. Dan was a child very attentive to detail. He loved to play with his toy soldiers using my recliner chair as an overhang, and he got along well with his playmates.

The children enrolled in Holy Name of Mary School in La Verne, and all of them excelled in their studies. The school was staffed by the Sisters of Saint Louis and several lay teachers.

Since my early childhood, chess has always been an appealing game, probably because I used to watch my father set up his board and spend hours in study. When I was very young, he spent whatever time necessary to teach me the fundamentals and proceeded to play many games with me. He enjoyed talking to me about Paul Morphy, who was born in New Orleans and who at one time had been the world champion. In fact, long ago, Morphy had lived on Chartres Street right around the corner from our house in what is now called the Beauregard House. Besides General Beauregard and Paul Morphy, another famous inhabitant of this house in years past was Frances Parkinson Keyes, the writer.

For the longest time, I could never beat Daddy at chess, but by persistent effort, I continued to learn. Then, occasionally, I was able to win a game when my father must have had other things on his mind. When I was away from home in the navy, I played a game with him by mail and managed to eke out a victory.

When our ship was preparing to move an army contingent during one of the phases of our Pacific campaign, there was the usual activity attendant to the loading of equipment and troops. However, some extra excitement existed, because this group let it be known that they had with them the chess champion of the division or something or other. They wanted to find a challenger and show off their champion. I found

Vestigia

the whole idea amusing and uninteresting. It so happened that my name came into prominence and it became a sort of obligation for me to accept a challenge for the navy.

When time permitted aboard ship, my adversary and I were isolated and we proceeded to play a game. It wasn't a pushover, but I managed to beat him. When the army troops aboard got this information, they were stunned. Obviously something must have gone wrong and another game would surely restore normality.

Next day, we went at it again, and once more I came out victorious. Puzzled by what he considered unorthodox play, my opponent walked away in disbelief.

On the third day, when the same results were again announced, I began to receive significant respect. I was ready to quit the match at any time, but obviously that would not have been the proper thing to do.

Since our trip was fairly long and we had several days yet to travel, we continued our games. My opponent announced that he thought he had figured out my technique. Indeed, he had! During the next few days, we played four more games, and I lost all four of them. Thus, I lost the series four to three.

After the war, I pursued my interest in chess and began to study; I joined a chess club and encountered some formidable opponents. My approach was obviously too intense, because I often felt like I had developed a fever and my sleep was beset with the night-long review of the games. I became interested in the lives of the grand masters and replayed some of their games. One man in particular whom I admired was Isaac Kashdan, the chess columnist for the *Los Angeles Times* newspaper. Sometime around 1930, there was an international tournament that was won by the world champion, a man named Alexander Alekhine. In this tournament, Kashdan placed second and thus gained the title of International Grandmaster.

Our club was quite active and arranged to have Kashdan come to play simultaneous chess with us. We provided twenty-one opponents, who paid $2.50 each for the privilege. When a chess master plays simultaneous chess, each challenger brings his own set and plays the black pieces. It is understood that the champion, having the white pieces, gets the first move, and he goes from board to board successively making his moves. He is not under any time constraint, but when he arrives at your board, you must make your move immediately.

I had spent considerable time in study before this match. Particularly, I learned the Caro Khan defense, which was a solid approach but not too often used. That was to be my weapon.

When play got underway, I followed my plan. Kashdan spent little time in deciding his move each time he came around to my table. It was obvious that a man of his caliber would have no problem whatsoever in handling this line of play. On the fifth move, however, I stumbled into difficulty when I inadvertently deviated from the prescribed course of action. Need I say more?—that's all you have to do in order to lose a game when you're playing at this level. In a total of thirty-two moves, I was history. I learned from my study and from this encounter that great chess players have a phenomenal memory and possess a keen analytical mind.

I moved up in the organization at General Dynamics. At times I was a Design Engineer, an Electronics Engineer, a Senior Electronics Engineer, an Assistant Group Engineer, a Section Head, and a Staff Engineer. All of our work was government funded, and as such it was subject to the political control of defense spending. When fears of national security prevailed, our funding was apt to go up; at other times, it could bottom out.

When we think of religious vocations in our family, we are particularly blessed. Mike was the last in this group. His response to this calling brings the Holy Sacrifice of the Mass into the midst of our family. I was greatly saddened when my responsibilities at home prevented me from attending his ordination in San Antonio. The members of the family who made the trip were: my mother and father, my brothers Albert and Louis, and Albert's five children: Albert III, Kathleen, Arthur, Thomas and Mary Ann. On June 1, 1957, during a very bad rain spell, the Sacrament of Holy Orders was conferred by Most Rev. Stephen A. Leven, D.D., and Mike's first solemn Mass was at the St. Louis Cathedral on Sunday, June 9th, at twelve o'clock.

Ann, our last child, was born on the 11th of November, 1959, exactly ten years after her brother Francis. I called her "Sweetie Babe." She had a rough time as an infant and required constant care. So often we needed a nurse in our home, and sure enough, we had one, a good one! When Ann was an infant, she was extremely irritable, and like her brother Steve, her problem was due to an inguinal hernia. To correct this situation, I spoke to a surgeon friend of mine who was the medical doctor at my job (General Dynamics in Pomona, California). Dr. Smith had retired from surgery because of a heart condition, but he agreed to do this surgery for me. Since he didn't have a surgical office to perform a pre-op examination, he came to the house. Linda witnessed Ann being examined and immediately piped up with, "Oh, Mommy, I have one of those lumps, too." Therefore, on the scheduled day, Dr. Smith did similar surgery on both girls. A bit unusual, I would say.

I remained in the Naval Reserve, and for months I took correspondence courses to maintain my status. After a while, I gave up this idea and fell into inactivity as far as my naval career was concerned.

I was honored by the City of La Verne when I was selected and approved by the City Council to become a member of the Planning Commission. I had been nominated by Leo Lomeli, a parishioner, who was a member of the City Council. I enjoyed serving as a commissioner for many months and received a proclamation from the city upon my departure from that post in 1961, when Marion's illness precluded further service.

Chapter Eight

Disguised Grace

With our six children in La Verne, our house was full, but it was adequate for our needs. We were able to keep up with current expenses, and I could see the light at the end of the tunnel.

I felt that disaster had befallen me when Marion was diagnosed with cancer in 1960. This era of my life was so traumatic and actually so filled with grace that in later years I was moved to write a book to share my blessings with those who would be so inclined to listen. Father Aloysius Ellacuria, CMF, was a very special spiritual director for Marion and me at this time. He was always available to us for guidance and prayer.

As Marion grew ill, I tried to resign my commission in the navy, but they informed me that I couldn't do that. They would have to be the one to offer that possibility. A few days later, I received a letter from the navy asking me if I would like to resign my commission. That I did. They got their way, and I got mine.

For fifteen months, Marion dealt with cancer after her mastectomy. Through radiation and chemotherapy she persevered nobly, setting an example of patience and acceptance of God's will. Not until Judgment Day will we truly know the tremendous good that she accomplished.

Marion suffered very much and had a resurgence of health several times due to the Blessings of Father Aloysius. Johnnie Lee Davis, a young girl of about 18 who had been one of Gertrude's charges at Maryvale Orphanage, came to live with us and gave us much needed help.

Each of the children had the opportunity to share their time with Marion. Ann was just a baby, and we would put her in bed with Marion where she played with Marion's radio. When Marion asked her what it was, she called it the "la la."

When Marion died in my arms in Pomona Valley Hospital on February 12, 1962, I had the terrible ordeal of going home to tell the six children. Of course it was extremely difficult to tell each one of them this shattering news. Then, as I assessed the level of comprehension of the four oldest children and the little comprehension had by Ann, the youngest, I was faced with the most difficult task: I had to tell Dan, who was almost four and a half at the time, that his mother was gone. That was heart wrenching.

Our family still maintained frequent contact with Father Aloysius, and he willingly shared his time with us. On August 22, 1962, Father gave me a copy of a special prayer book. During the preceding months, he had given us several books, but this book was different. This was a daily prayer book. It was *The Little Office of the Blessed Virgin Mary*. It became my daily prayer forever after. When the book wore out, I had it redone either by photocopy or by retyping the text. When computers and scanners came into vogue, I was able to put them to good use on this project. I never wanted to buy a new version of this book because it would change the phraseology, and the old text was firmly rooted in my mind.

My book entitled *My Guide* was written in 1986. It was self-published and made available for several years in hardcopy, free of charge. A Claretian priest in Bilbao, Spain, Father Javier Oroz, CMF, wrote and asked me for permission to translate and publish this book in Spain. I gladly acceded to his request. *Our Guide* was translated into Spanish and published in Spain by the Claretian Fathers. The publisher was Euskalerriko Klaretarrak, Secretaria Provincial, San Francisco, 14, 6.º, 48003 Bilbao, Spain. Several years later, in the interest of economy, I had the English version printed in paperback form and again distributed it free of charge. My intention was to acquaint as many people as possible with the wonders of God's grace. Then, on September 13, 1996, Patricia Treece wrote about Father Aloysius in *The Tidings*, the Los Angeles diocesan newspaper, and cited my book as a reference. With the calls that ensued from this publicity, I had to have additional copies printed, and at that time I sold them.

At one time I was asked to explain the role of Father Aloysius in "my unusual response to suffering" and why "I have devotion to a man whose prayers failed to cure my wife." I said that I sincerely believe that my response to suffering is not unusual. So many, many people have intense suffering far beyond what has befallen me, and their responses to the challenges are so meritorious and so exemplary that it truly puts me to shame.

Every day I run into people who have been given much less than I, and their investment of their gifts has reaped bountiful harvests. If I

Vestigia

keep my eyes focused on these souls, then maybe I can produce some yield. Many such giants have been intimately involved in my life, and they inspire me to recall the Preface of the Saints: "They spur us on to victory…"

Also, I must say that Father Aloysius's prayers did not fail to cure my wife. To be granted a physical cure, which of its very nature is time-limited, is of lesser value than the "eternal cure," which I saw manifest in her. It was she, who had little formal religious education, who inspired me, upon whom the Lord had lavished His spiritual indoctrination, to attend daily Mass. No better example of the acceptance of suffering could have been given to me than the one that she demonstrated. It seems as though the Lord wished to inform us of the difference between this spiritual cure and the physical one when He intermittently cured her during her illness.

After Marion died, I raised the children with the help of various generous people such as Hilda Jacobs and Johnnie Lee Davis. During this era, Linda was an absolute Godsend. She worked around the house and took motherly care of her siblings.

Gail followed the trend of her peers as a teenager and took to modern music. Fortunately, her musical preference was not of the wild variety. She enjoyed the songs of Neil Diamond, and if it were not for Gail, I never would have heard of this man.

When Gail got word of a future Neil Diamond concert at the Greek Theater, she wrote to his manager and asked for a copy of the program for her collection. She mentioned that she would be unable to attend because she had no transportation, but she wanted a copy of the program if possible. I was unaware of this request, but I soon found out the result. Gail came to me one day and said that she had heard from the manager and that she was invited to go to the concert and also to go backstage after the show to meet Neil. I guess you might say that the Greek Theater was not exactly around the corner, and the parking area was surely not designed with parking in mind, but no minor difficulties like these could keep us away—I was as excited as she was. Gail convinced me that the music would be acceptable and not offensive to my ears.

We went to this concert, and both of us thoroughly enjoyed it. After the show, even though there were many people crowding around at the entrance to the stage area, we were allowed backstage without any difficulty. Soon, Neil Diamond appeared and began to chat with Gail. Fortunately, I had brought my instant camera and took the opportunity to ask if I could take a shot of him with Gail. He readily consented. After taking a couple of pictures, we were ready to go. However, there was another girl nearby who saw my success with the camera and pleaded with me to do the same for her. When I explained that I had no power to make that decision, she asked Neil if it would be possible. Again he happily agreed to the request, and I clicked the camera once more. In identical fashion, another girl caught sight of us and pleaded her case for a picture. Somewhere along the line, this operation had to come to a halt, not because of any reluctance on the part of Neil Diamond but because I had run out of film. Every time I reminisce about this event in Gail's life, I enjoy the whole thing all over again, because I was able to share something meaningful with her.

I continued to prosper in my job, and I was given greater responsibility. I became a Group Engineer and directed the testing and evaluation of all engineering and experimental missiles. When I progressed to Section Head in the Documentation Department, even though I had the responsibility of seventy-six employees, I chose to take on the additional task of teaching Shop Mathematics at night for a semester at Mount San Antonio Junior College in Walnut, California.

At this time, the Electronics Division in Rochester, New York, was seeking to increase its staff, and a representative came to California to recruit me. Our discussion went favorably, and they flew me to Rochester to be interviewed by each of the department heads. A few days later I was offered a position with that division. This was to be a significant promotion, and this transfer to Rochester meant taking charge of their documentation section and the responsibility for similar facilities that they had in San Diego and Orlando, Florida. I would now have two hundred employees and a geographical challenge. It was company policy to defray the moving expense, but so many other intangibles made me really ponder such a move. There would be an enormous responsibility with a modest increase in pay. I prayed for guidance. When I turned down the offer, I never really knew until several months later how great was the answer to my prayer. That division folded! They did it without me!

For several months, I worked with a special team on a major proposal for possible future funding. If this contract were to be granted, it would provide an enormous lift to the sagging financial situation that now existed in our company. Unfortunately, our proposal was not accepted.

Vestigia

On June 10, 1969, my birthday, the bottom fell out. I was laid off from General Dynamics after having worked there for twelve and a half years. Funding for major programs had declined, and that situation always starts heads rolling.

Chapter Nine

Mary Naughten

*I*t wasn't until 1969 that I met Mary Elizabeth Naughten of Claremont, California, through Katherine Morrow. Katherine knew Marion, Katherine knew Mary, and she also knew Father Aloysius. She knew everybody. She had a heart of gold. I can't say enough good things about her.

I dated Mary for about four months, during which time we visited Father Aloysius. Father was very pleased that we were dating. He wondered when we were going to get married and advised us to do so. Most specifically, he gave us this advice right after one of our visits to him on Westchester Place. We walked through the hallway, closed the door, and were just about to descend the stairs when he re-opened the door a little bit and put his head through to recite to us a portion of scripture that Mary and I alone had been discussing on our way to his residence. God indeed does act in strange ways.

It was only by a favorable contact and, of course, many prayers that I finally got a new job in August of the same year at Aerojet in Azusa, California, working on surveillance satellites. This job, just like the previous ones, was fascinating. I was placed in charge of a test group whose responsibility was to verify the acceptance of electronic assemblies for use in the satellites that we were making for the U.S. Air Force.

Mary and I were married by Father William Condon at Holy Name of Mary Church in La Verne on September 24, 1969, the feast of Our Lady of Ransom. I jokingly said that I married Mary for her money. In reality, her job and medical benefits from Kaiser Steel provided much-needed assistance to our family. Mary brought with her the element of parental guidance and upbringing that I could not possibly give by myself, and she integrated into a family of six children who knew only their father as the one with authority. God chose two separate mothers for my children; forever I will be grateful for these two blessings.

Sometimes I had to travel. On one of the trips, I made it my business to stop in New Orleans to visit Daddy and Mother. Right before leaving New Orleans, I stopped at the Acme Oyster House for about two dozen raw oysters. After I boarded the plane for home, it took only about two hours for me to get very ill. Once I made it home, I went right to bed. The next day, the doctor knew immediately that I had food poisoning when I told him what I had eaten in New Orleans. I don't remember ever again eating those delicious raw oysters from the Gulf of Mexico.

Soon after I was employed, the government cancelled the work for which I had been hired, and the prevailing contracts were my only means of survival. In subsequent weeks, our proposal for new work was rewarded with contracts that were very beneficial to my men and me. We were given the responsibility for performing radiation testing of the electronic assemblies that were a part of the surveillance satellite that we made.

In 1971 or 1972, I journeyed to San Francisco, Seattle, San Diego, and Owego, New York, to evaluate gamma radiation facilities suitable for our testing. My first evaluation was the bremsstrahlung facility of the Boeing Aircraft Company in Seattle. On the first leg of my trip, when I had finished my tour in mid-afternoon, I left the Boeing facility to check into my hotel. Pretty soon I found out that if I could change my plans, I could do something really exciting. I was scheduled to leave Seattle the next morning to fly to Syracuse and then switch to Mohawk Airlines for a flight to Binghamton; from Binghamton, I would drive to Owego to visit IBM. But now I could see the opportunity to change my scheduled flight and take my first trip in a Boeing 747 plane, a design recently put into service. In spite of the inconvenience that it entailed, I changed my plans to take this flight in place of the one I had booked. I checked out of the hotel immediately, without spending one night in it. I went to the Seattle-Tacoma airport and caught the 747 for Chicago. This new plane was everything I had hoped it would be. At Chicago I changed to a conventional plane and continued to Syracuse, where I arrived at six in the morning. Here I received a double whammy: it had been ten degrees above zero shortly before landing, and the Mohawk Airline was on strike. The task that I faced now, after a self-imposed sleepless night, was to drive all the way down highway 80 in New York, past the snow banks, to Binghamton. Thanks be to God, He heard my prayers and got me there safely, in spite of the buildup of ice under my fenders as I drove through the cold morning.

Vestigia

When I had visited the IBM facility and completed my tour, I was ready to get a hotel for much-needed sleep. However, the weather prediction frightened me. A blizzard was forecast for that afternoon, and I was afraid that I would be marooned for days in Binghamton unless I escaped right away. Since there was no flight possible to Syracuse because of the airline strike and I knew I would have to drive, I decided to get started. That I did, but I was tired—too tired. Soon after I started this longer-than-100-mile drive, I knew I was in trouble with fatigue. We are told to pull off the road in such cases and take a rest, but I was afraid to do so. I thought the blizzard would begin and completely inundate me and that maybe I wouldn't be seen for days. So I drove and I drove. I was so tired that my only method of staying awake was to put the radio up to high volume, open the window, and keep praying and screaming. I knew if I didn't do all of these things, I'd fall asleep. It seemed like no one was on the road but me, and it was cold. For hours I drove past the snow drifts. Fortunately, I did not detect any snow or ice on the pavement, but it was a most painful trip. Because God had pity on my exploits, He got me to Syracuse safely. Since that day, I try not to do things that are so risky.

After I chose the most propitious locations to perform our test program, I saw to it that contracts were awarded to the appropriate laboratories for our use. Then, in the following months, I took crews of engineers to these places to perform the necessary tests. These tests were designed to demonstrate the ability of the circuits to withstand simulated nuclear-generated radiation. The daily rate to use the facilities for which we contracted was sometimes as high as a thousand dollars. I had to keep these costs as low as possible so that we would not overrun our contract. In one case I went to Seattle one day, did some testing, returned to Azusa that night with a failed circuit, and got it into the hands of the designers. It was redesigned and repaired that night, and I returned with it the next morning to Seattle for verification testing.

One day in La Verne, Mary received a jury duty summons from the Los Angeles County Superior Court. After I left for work in Azusa, she drove to Los Angeles. Upon arrival, she was told that they were seeking to form a jury for a forthcoming trial, and the nature of this trial was such that no one was to speak a thing about it once outside of the court house. This was the instruction given by Judge Alarcon.

Day after day Mary drove in to the court for the jury selection process. Obediently, she followed the court's instruction and told me almost nothing. All that I knew was that sometimes two or three potential members had been chosen, and then on another day one or two of these had been removed. I couldn't tell whether they were making any progress in selecting twelve members for a jury.

There was a big espionage case that was in the works at this time, so I assumed it possible that Mary would be selected for this trial.

Several days went by, and each evening upon her arrival home, the only information that Mary had for me was the current number of jurors that were seated. Finally, she announced one evening that the trial had begun and that she had been sworn in as a juror. Day after day the trial progressed and she journeyed back and forth daily to Los Angeles, about thirty-five miles each way.

Then one day when I arrived home, Gail told me that the bailiff at the court house had called to tell me that Mary had been sequestered and that I should go to such and such a hotel at six that evening to bring her some clothes. I still didn't know what the nature of the trial was—but now I knew that the jury had been sequestered.

A few days later I had to take a trip to Seattle for the radiation testing program. As I stood in line at the Ontario, California, airport reading the morning paper, my eyes locked on a column on the front page. It drew my attention because it talked about Judge Alarcon and a sequestered jury. Those were the only two things that I knew about Mary's jury duty. I learned that this case involved the Manson family's attempt to break Charles Manson, a notorious murderer, out of prison. Because two jurors were excused from duty when they had received threats on their lives and the lives of their families, the judge immediately acted to safeguard his remaining jurors. He sequestered the jury and ordered that their families be protected. Now, I was on my way to Seattle as I had planned, but there was a peculiar situation at hand, since the lives of the jurors' families were being threatened. As soon as the opportunity arose, I called the court and complained about the fact that everybody knew about the threats except me—I wasn't allowed to know. It was even more disturbing to realize that during the interrogation of prospective jurors, the team for the defendants had learned many things about each juror and their families. Everything about us was an open book to the perpetrators. I was told that my local police department was safeguarding our house. I wasn't satisfied until I verified this fact in detail by calling my police department.

Vestigia

After fifteen days of sequestration, the trial and penalty phase were completed and our home was back to normal. I did, however, harbor fear of retribution on our family. It took me many months to become convinced that the possible reprisal period for this trial was over. It surely was opportune that we chose during this time to make our move from La Verne to Alta Loma.

When the radiation testing program was completed, I worked in a staff capacity for the design and procurement of a critical element of our system. There was a company in Boston that manufactured a focal plane assembly that was part of our satellite system, and periodic meetings were held there to track the manufacturing progress. When the time came that a particular segment of this assembly was ready for delivery to us, I was sent to Boston as a courier for the unit. Because of its classification, I had a particular routine to follow. I had a rather large, hermetically sealed suitcase-type container that weighed about twenty pounds. This "suitcase" was to be with me at all times, never to be opened by anyone, and it had to be at my side in an adjacent seat in the airplane. To handle a container of this size meant that I required two seats in first-class—one for me and one for the suitcase.

I arrived in Boston on schedule, picked up the container as planned, and returned to Logan Field to catch the flight back to Los Angeles. The airline was alerted to my specific requirements and took good care of me. Since I had an hour or so to wait at the airport, TWA put me in a special room alone where I watched the Watergate hearings on television. I was oblivious of the outside world until my program was interrupted by an announcement that there was a plane crash at Logan Field in Boston. "That's me," I said to myself. I looked out the window and couldn't see a thing; the fog was thick and the field was shut down. I learned that a plane had crashed in the fog at the end of the runway and almost a hundred lives were lost.

Now I was marooned at the airport with this precious cargo. When I called my company for instructions, they let me know that I was on my own and I could do whatever I thought best. I could even return the unit to the safety of the facility that made it and start out again the next day. I didn't want that! I decided to stay put as long as necessary. It was now TWA's job to continue taking care of me. They kept me isolated and brought me whatever I requested. Hour after hour rolled by, and the fog never cleared all day.

Finally at six o'clock TWA notified me that I should board the plane. To my surprise, a few people were already seated as I claimed my two places in first class. In a moment, the black lady behind me spoke and wanted to know if I was a musician—she thought my big suitcase contained a musical instrument, and I guess I looked important being in first class with two seats. I let her know that I had no instrument with me and if I were to have one, it would be a small clarinet. Besides, I really wasn't a musician. Thus began a nice cross-country acquaintance with Ella Fitzgerald. She spoke of her music and her family and discussed New Orleans and its reputation for music and food. She couldn't remember the name of her favorite dish but said that I should go to the Fairmont Roosevelt and ask them to serve me the seafood that Ella likes. Then she wanted me to call her and let her know how I liked it.

For years she has been famous for singing "A Tisket a Tasket, I Lost My Yellow Basket," and I asked her if she ever gets tired of people requesting this song. She was impressive in her reply, saying that she was glad to sing it if it made people happy.

The airline saw to it that I disembarked first. After a long tiresome day, it was good to be back in Los Angeles. All I had to do now was get to my company and lock this big thing up in the safe. When I got to the street and headed for my car, I heard a voice call to me. There was Ella, shouting out of her Rolls Royce, offering to give me a ride. I thanked her and said I'd like that very much but that it was necessary for me to go my own way at this time.

It was then that I was placed on special assignment covering the sunshades used on our surveillance satellite unit. These shades were designed to protect the delicate, optically sensitive assemblies of the satellite from the powerful rays of the sun. When the rocket system is fired, it carries the satellite into orbit. After arriving in orbit, it is the proper function of the system to turn downward toward the earth for its correct viewing position. As such, the sunshades must be explosively blown away to allow a clear view of the potential target area. My assignment was to follow the history of the explosive bolts used for this operation and determine their shelf life so that the current warehouse of satellites would continue to be flight worthy.

Now, it became obvious that our home in La Verne was not adequate, and we were blessed in finding a fine dwelling at 7124 Hellman Ave. in Alta Loma. We bought this home on the Feast of the Annunciation, March 25, 1973. This place was a bonanza, but it has required continuous care due to its size and the number of trees. Initially we had about nineteen fruit trees. From time to time we have cut some of these down and replanted others.

Alta Loma is situated just two miles south of the San Gabriel Mountains. These lofty peaks give a splendid view to the north, and when they are snowcapped they are awesome. One Thanksgiving morning after breakfast, Mary and I decided to take a trip up Mount Baldy Road, where the snowfall of the previous night had made the mountains very inviting. There were almost no cars on the road, so we were comfortably taking in the scenery as we ventured higher and higher. Suddenly, a highway patrolman stopped us and said we couldn't proceed any farther without chains. Not having any, we made a U-turn and headed back down the mountain. After going just a couple hundred yards, we came to a curve in the road where I lightly tapped the brakes. That's when I got into a whole mess of trouble. We began to skid violently down the mountain, totally out of control. I tried to remember the emergency procedure that I was taught—turn into the direction of the skid. I don't think I was able to achieve anything at all, but I did pray! We finally came to a stop at a curve, just a few feet from the edge of the road. In retrospect, I realized that we had been the victims of "black ice"—a thin layer of ice invisibly coating the asphalt road, making it slick as glass.

In 1974, while I was working at Aerojet, I embarked on a physical fitness program on my own. Essentially, I devoted my efforts to two exercises: pushups and jogging in place. I was determined to perform the pushups perfectly and increase the number of them gradually. When I began, I was able to do only a few, maybe eight or ten. Systematically I pursued my plan over a period of many weeks. One day I peaked out at 102 pushups, and I felt that I had reached my goal. Soon thereafter, I developed a severely pinched nerve in my neck that required hospitalization with traction for several days. Supposedly, this affliction was not due to my exercise, but I'll never believe that.

As in all other government-funded jobs, the task at Aerojet, too, came to completion, and I was again laid off in August of 1975. In December 1975, by concerted effort and constant prayer, I was able to procure employment with the Hughes Aircraft Corporation in Irvine, California. I never wanted to work in this area because it was too far from home in a heavily congested traffic area. It entailed a drive each way of about fifty miles, most of which was on freeways. Not having any choice, since there were no other offers, I began work for Hughes and through the next eight years was adequately compensated. We were able to pay off our house and maintain equity.

At this time, the Department of Consumer Affairs of the State of California effected some changes in their regulations for granting Professional Engineering licenses. One of the significant changes pertinent to me was the adoption of a grandfather clause in the field of Quality Engineering. By virtue of this new regulation, I was granted a license after I presented the proper affidavits. The title of Quality Engineer was most appropriate, since I had worked through the years in so many different phases of engineering and my job now required that I maintain quality control in numerous production processes.

Commuting to Irvine, however, was a memorable experience. In fact, it was one experience after another; particularly, I looked upon the big rigs on the road as my nemeses. To illustrate the potential hazard that I faced, I remember the morning that I was going west on the Riverside Freeway directly behind a large vehicle transport truck that was carrying about eight smaller trucks. Each of these trucks had a large spare wheel attached to its back end. Suddenly, I noticed that the last truck had lost its spare wheel, which now began to fall from a height of about ten feet. It hit the ground about fifty feet directly in front of me and bounced up in the air. I was forced to make an immediate decision: should I slow down and swerve to avoid a collision, or should I speed up and attempt to drive under the trajectory? Not having any time for deliberation, I immediately stepped on the gas as hard as I could, and with that acceleration, I fit right under the arc of this wild wheel. I know that it was my urgent prayer that saved my life. Many years later, I learned that Doug Yegge, a close friend of mine, had been traveling west one day in that same time frame on the same road when he was confronted with a wheel on the road right ahead of him. He could not avoid the resultant collision, which took out the underside of his car. His vehicle was totaled. Most probably, Doug smashed into the wheel that I had avoided.

In October of 1979, Mary and I made a trip to Europe; we began our journey in Los Angeles on the Feast of the Holy Rosary and landed in Madrid. We wanted to go there first because the Basilica of Our Lady of Pilar was nearby in the city of Saragossa. During the first century, St. James the Apostle had been assigned to preach in that area and

Vestigia

was experiencing difficulty. Our Blessed Lady came with her assistance. The Basilica, the first Marian Shrine, was erected to commemorate this visit, and thus I had attached great significance to this memorial. As soon as we entered that huge basilica, Mary suggested that we look among the many altars and find the Blessed Sacrament. As soon as we did so, we noticed that a priest was just about to begin Mass. I don't know what nationality he was, but I thought I should serve the Mass. I did a creditable job until it came time for the ablution. The wine poured badly over the lip of the cruet, and the water did likewise. Later, at the second ablution, the same problem occurred. I spilled the water on the floor. There just seemed to be no way to corral the flow from those cruets.

Right after Mass, I resolved to do something about this problem; it would fulfill my desire to make a donation in honor of Our Lady. We went out to buy some new cruets, but no one understood what we were looking for. It took most of the day to deal with this situation. It was only through the assistance of a woman who came by and spoke perfect English and Spanish that we were able to solve this problem. She was there, I'm sure, in answer to our prayers. We procured durable metal cruets and brought them back to the church. I'd like to believe that they are still serving their purpose.

We spent nineteen days visiting Spain, France, Italy, and Ireland. Our main intention for this trip was to make a pilgrimage. We met this goal in Spain by visiting Our Lady of Pilar Shrine in Saragossa; in France, we spent three days at the shrine of Lourdes; in Rome, we spent a week visiting the many beautiful and holy edifices such as St. Peter's, Santa Maria Maggiore, St. John Lateran, the Colosseum, etc. A comfortable aspect of the journey was the last few days of the pilgrimage, which were spent in Ireland. Here they spoke English, and we no longer had to struggle in order to communicate. However, I did find it extremely difficult to adapt to the driving regulations. When we rented a car and drove from Dublin through Athlone (the birthplace of Mary's father) and on to Galway, we had to drive on the left side of the road and our steering wheel was on the right side of the car. Additionally, all of the roads were very narrow, and the street signs were often placed on buildings at the corners of the streets. At Knock, we visited the venerable Shrine of Our Lady, but I wasn't greatly impressed. In a visit to the same shrine eleven years later, I became more informed and came away with a much greater devotion.

It was about 1981 when we ventured to Hawaii. We stayed on Oahu, where I had been twice before while I was in the navy. I still remembered the slogan that I first heard in 1944: "Truly the land where you can't remember what you came to forget." It is hard to describe the beauty of these islands, and the music that has been written for this scenery is most appealing.

During this era, we also made a four-day roundtrip from San Pedro to Ensenada on one of the cruise lines. It was very enjoyable and fulfilled my dream of making an ocean voyage unencumbered by navy duty. We particularly enjoyed the opportunity of attending Mass at a local church in Ensenada, where the children were preparing for their First Holy Communion. These kinds of trips are great, but you have to be careful because the food is stupendous.

My parent's wedding anniversary is on August 14th; this is a very uncomfortable time of the year in New Orleans because of the heat and humidity. Whenever possible, we tried to visit them at this time. Sometimes, my brother Joe would also be there. I believe that he suffered from the heat as much as I did, because we each attempted to outdo the other in gaining a choice position in front of the fan. It was a comical sight to see him walk around the house with a towel wrapped around his head to provide additional relief from the heat.

On August 20, 1981, my father died suddenly. In a few months he would have been eighty-nine. We gathered at the St. Louis Cathedral Church for his funeral. At the Mass that he celebrated, Mike spoke eloquently, but it was impossible to describe a man who was indescribable. Daddy had never hesitated to portray his beliefs when called upon to do so in public. He was an extremely energetic, learned, pedagogic Catholic layman. Because I lived with him and observed him closely, I knew that he was a man who practiced what he preached. There was a period of time when he had made over thirty consecutive annual retreats with the Jesuits at Manresa in Convent, Louisiana. He assisted very often as Retreat Captain. I am proud to be his son.

Mary and I strive to serve our diocese in whatever way we are able. We were appointed as Extraordinary Ministers of the Eucharist at Sacred Heart Church. We made use of this wonderful blessing by serving at Sunday Masses and by bringing Holy Communion to the sick. Here is an incident involving this ministry:

Ever since 1962, I had infrequent migraine headaches. More often than not, there was no actual pain involved, but my vision was always severely limited. One Sunday, while serving as a Eucharistic Minister and kneeling at Communion time, I had one of these attacks. Because of the acute vision problem that I had, I knew that I could not safely distribute Holy Communion. Immediately I gave the problem to Our Lord and let Him know that I needed help. Immediate was His response—my problem disappeared! Many years later, in the same capacity as Eucharistic Minister at St. Peter and St. Paul church in Alta Loma, it was also at Communion time that I had a difficult situation. While standing at the altar, I felt so bad that I knew I couldn't trust myself to last another minute—I needed help. Once again I pleaded to God for assistance. Immediately, a man who was not a Eucharistic Minister came up from the congregation and stood beside me. I didn't ask him for help, and all of a sudden I did not need it. My problem disappeared instantly. "Mysteriously," then, the man went back to his place. Mass continued.

On June 1, 1984, after years of strenuous commuting, I was forced to retire from Hughes. My back had become so afflicted with arthritis and herniated discs that sleeping for more than an hour at a time in a regular bed became very painful. I discovered that a reclining lounge chair alleviated the pain considerably and also provided a means for sleep. I'm sure that pain killers or the anti-inflammatory drugs that the doctor offered would also have been helpful, but I avoided drugs as much as possible. As it was, I was taking blood pressure medicine as a regular routine, and I wanted to hold it at that.

During the following weeks, I was contacted by Hughes and offered a job as a consultant. Since the pay was generous and I was allowed to select the hours of work to diminish the stress of commuting, I gladly took the opportunity. It was significant that precisely at this time, Father Joseph Snoj, a dear friend at Sacred Heart Church in nearby Etiwanda, began to suffer acutely from the effects of degeneration of the macula. With only peripheral vision, it became impossible for him to say Mass without assistance. In cases of this nature, the Canon Law of the Church allows a priest to be assisted at Mass. Canon 930:(2) states: "A priest who is blind or suffering from some other infirmity may lawfully celebrate the Eucharistic Sacrifice by using the text of any approved Mass, with the assistance, if need be, of another priest or deacon or even a properly instructed lay person." Thus I became a privileged person to assist Father Snoj by reading the Gospel and prompting him during Mass with the words of the special prayers for the day. I was able to perform this function both in his private chapel and in the main church. Many times, Mary, too, helped him in his chapel. Soon thereafter, I was instrumental in getting similar assistance for him from our son Steve and two other laymen. With reduced hours of work because of my consulting status, I was able to help Father practically any time that he needed it.

For Maxine's fiftieth anniversary as a Daughter of Charity, many of us gathered in St. Louis for the occasion. Mother was in festive spirits at this celebration, and she provided us with endless humor. Gertrude's fiftieth anniversary in Austin brought us together again for another joyful reunion. We celebrated Muriel's fiftieth at the St. Louis Cathedral School in New Orleans. What a wonderful location for each of us during this auspicious occasion.

My assignments at Hughes continued to be interesting and challenging. Even in the midst of problems there was always a moment available for humor, as was the case during one of our investigations.

A rather complicated assembly had exhibited failure when put to use by one of our customers. The customer's diagnosis indicated a mode of failure that I did not agree with—the theory seemed far-fetched. It was proposed that we perform an operational test and employ a very high speed movie camera to document the explosive operation of our assembly. The timing for this test had to be precise, because the intensity of the light produced great heat, and the rate of photography, which was several thousand frames per second, meant that the reel of film lasted for about two seconds. Because of these constraints, we had numerous repeats of the test. Each time, a new reel of film had to be loaded. I saved one of these reels that had been used but not developed.

After a successful test had been made and documented, it gave conclusive evidence that the conjecture that had been made by our customer had been correct and I had been absolutely wrong. These frame-by-frame pictures slowed down the whole explosive operation and thus proved the point. Now that we were certain of the nature of the problem, it became easy enough to solve the design failure.

When I drove back to the engineering department to submit the test results and conclusion, the Chief Engineer was anxiously awaiting my report, for he had heard nothing yet. I hastened to tell him of the great difficulty and expense that was involved in performing this test but did not give him the data—I pretended that it was undeveloped in the film can under my arm. I assured him that we knew that we had performed a successful test and merely had to develop the movie to learn the results. When he was convinced of the tremendous value of my film, I proceeded with my planned maneuver to approach his desk and accidentally have the can fall to the floor, spilling its contents, such that the reel of undeveloped film rolled across the office, exposing it to obvious ruin. His shocked reaction was immediate but short lived—it didn't take long for him to spot my trick!

Our daughter Ann repeatedly advised me to get a computer, because she knew I would enjoy it. I continually fought off the suggestion until I was presented with a secondhand unit from a friend. From that time onward, I was addicted. I made it my business to study the system and procure whatever help I needed. In fact, I relished writing programs and actually wrote many of them using the Quick Basic language.

I remember what a revelation the handheld calculator had been to my father when I showed him that we could read logarithms to seven decimal places. Present-day computer technology would have been absolutely ideal for him.

Chapter Ten

Retirement

*I*n December of 1991, when the business fortunes of Hughes had changed significantly so that I was no longer needed, I again made the transition to retirement.

I began doing the things that one always dreams of doing in retirement. But soon I found out that I no longer had the physical ability to carry out all my plans. I enjoyed working in the yard and in the garage. One fruitful enterprise for me was the succession of video interviews that I undertook to document the life of Father Aloysius Ellacuria, CMF. In this project I was able to tape the stories of fifty people who had known him and had experienced his many blessings. If another book is to be written about this holy man, there is a lot of pertinent information available in these interviews. In order to provide greater assistance for such a book, I have begun to transcribe these interviews. Some of them are quite lengthy; when people are talking about something that is near and dear to them they are inclined to be wordy. It tends to be tricky, knowing when to steer the conversation into a different vein or to bring it to a conclusion. When I spoke to Patricia Treece, a renowned author, about this situation, she gave me some excellent advice. She said that I should be patient and let the commentary continue. She said that if I wait, some pertinent information will eventually come forth. I have tried this approach and found it to be quite profitable.

Heretofore, my brother Albert was never agreeable to an in-depth conversation about his wartime ordeal, but now he and his wife, Effie, drove out to see us in Alta Loma. I took them to the Chino Air Museum, where there was a B17G on display, just like Albert's old plane, the Flying Fortress. Right in front of this plane, I interviewed him and heard his heart-wrenching story in detail. Unfortunately, at this time the wind was howling, and my camera recorder picked up the noise. But I got the story.

My military service has been presented in an ongoing manner; perhaps here is a place to summarize it.

Francis X. Levy

I was affiliated with the U.S. Navy, either on active duty or reserve status, for eighteen and a half years. I am happy that I was able to serve my country, and I am most grateful to God for the many blessings that I received during this time.

A synopsis of my duty in the navy is as follows:

- Serial Number 384517 (as an officer), 5747629 (as an enlisted man).

- Enlisted in the navy on January 28, 1943. Was called to active duty in the V-12 Unit at Tulane University in New Orleans, Louisiana, on July 1, 1943, to pursue my standard college curriculum with additional naval studies.

- Transferred to pre-midshipmen school, Asbury Park, New Jersey, March 1944, to await assignment to midshipmen school.

- Transferred to Chicago, Illinois, by troop train and appointed Midshipman at Northwestern University, Chicago, Illinois, on June 16, 1944.

- Commissioned as an Ensign in the U.S. Naval Reserve on September 14, 1944, at Navy Pier in Chicago.

- Reported to the Administrative Command of the Amphibious Forces of the Pacific Fleet in Pearl Harbor, Hawaii, in October 1944.

- Assigned to serve aboard the LST-712 for duty in Pearl Harbor in October 1944.

- Participated in the invasion of Lingayen Gulf, Philippine Islands, January 9, 1945.

- Participated in the invasion of Okinawa, April 1, 1945.

- Transferred to LST-683, April 10, 1946.

Vestigia

- Transferred to New Orleans, Louisiana, for release to inactive duty on May 14, 1946.

- Released from active duty under honorable conditions on May 31, 1946.

- Joined the Military Sea Transportation Service (MSTS) Active Naval Reserve in New Orleans about 1949.

- Ordered to active duty on September 12, 1950, for the Korean War.

- Reported for active duty on October 2, 1950.

- Reported aboard LST-1101, November 1950, for the Korean War.

- Released to inactive duty, September 24, 1952, as a Lieutenant.

- Honorably Discharged from Naval Reserve on June 23, 1961.

Authorized to wear:
Philippine Liberation Medal
Asiatic-Pacific Theater Medal (2 Stars)
American Theater Medal
World War II Victory Medal
Japanese Occupation Medal
Korean Conflict Medal

••

I have maintained membership in the American Legion and kept in touch with some of my shipmates through the United States LST Association. In fact, Mary and I went to one of their reunions in New Orleans in 1991. I remembered my shipmates from the LST-712, but I couldn't recognize some of them. After all, it had been forty-five years since I had seen them.

A few years later, we were back in New Orleans at Mardi Gras time. Actually, the purpose of this trip was to see my brother Louis, who was quite ill. In all of the years that we were married, I had never taken Mary to Mardi Gras because I felt that it had deteriorated so drastically in later years that it had become abominable.

In my days in New Orleans, Mardi Gras was a special time because of the religious culture that exists there. Mardi Gras (Fat Tuesday) is the last day of the pre-Lenten season. It is also the last day of the Carnival season, which began on Twelfth Night—the twelfth night after Christmas. Therefore, Carnival is a season, and Mardi Gras is a day. This Carnival season varies in length from year to year because Ash Wednesday (the day that Lent begins) and Easter Sunday move in accordance with the lunar month. (Easter is the first Sunday after the first full moon after the vernal equinox).

When we were young, we always dressed in an appropriate costume for Mardi Gras, and we went together as a family to view the Rex parade from a protruding ledge on one of the downtown business buildings on Camp Street. It was a day of fun and excitement, and, of course, it is always a holiday. Now the situation has changed completely. Due to the debauchery that now prevails on Mardi Gras, I tell everyone it is the time to stay away from New Orleans.

The common belief is that the time of retirement is the time for travel. Well, I hold to that belief emphatically. Fortunately, we have made many trips, including St. Louis, San Antonio, and San Francisco. In addition to New Orleans, we enjoy the wine country of Napa Valley in California. This valley has given us an opportunity to learn a lot about the wine-making process and a chance to savor the natural beauty of the terrain. A special enjoyment here is a periodic visit to the wineries in both the Napa and Sonoma valleys. I believe the ambiance of this area is tops, and it is just what is needed for restful relaxation.

Perhaps when you grow up in an area of a city with houses close together, lacking any space between them so that they have common walls, you'll dream of the open spaces of the West. So many of our songs reflect this vision and have offered this appeal to me. One thing that I'm sure of is that there is an absolute difference between the music of my era and the "music" of today. In days gone by, especially during the forties and the fifties, the sounds were romantic, peaceful. The songs had melodies that lingered in our minds, and the lyrics that accompanied them were so appropriately suited: they reflected genius on

Vestigia

the part of their creators. For me, music is therapeutic, and I believe that it is that way for all, at least to some degree. However, the discord that I hear in some of the modern music symbolizes the distress that is found in today's society. All is not lost, however, for there are some melodious new compositions, though they be few and far between.

I never thought that I would ever spend much time in Mexico. I avoided it for many years until Mary and I visited Alamos, Sonora, for the ordinations of the Missionaries of Perpetual Adoration. This country presented a new vista for us.

In December 1996, Mary and I visited Patricia Andreu and her family in Aguascalientes, Mexico. We also spent a few days in Mexico City and went to the shrine of Our Lady of Guadalupe. I would recommend that site to anyone who wishes to visit a shrine of Our Lady. There is a "moving floor" that brings the visitors in front of the miraculous image. In this manner, they keep the people moving and prevent them from accumulating in one spot, blocking others from the view. We went around and around several times in order to see and photograph this magnificent tilma.

From 1995 through 1999, we made countless trips to Tecate, Mexico, to visit the Sisters of the Trinitarians of Mary. Mary's sister, Peggy, (Sister Margaret Mary) is a member of that order, and each trip is an opportunity to visit with her.

Several times a year we have been able to spend time in Ventura at the Buenaventura Mission. Whenever we are in that city, we stay overnight and make it our primary object to pray in Adoration at the mission. It is typical of the many missions of Father Junipero Serra here in California, but we like this one especially because of its many attractions for us. Aside from the opportunity for Adoration, Ventura presents a beautiful panorama of the Pacific. The space to park and the scenery to enjoy make this locale a very special place indeed.

We do not always see the answers to our prayers, even though we know that they are heard. One particular incident comes to mind in this regard. Our dear friend Father Frank Ambrosi came to town on one of his visits. He was always invigorating and a pure delight to have around; we cherished his visits. He was full of the Holy Spirit! On this occasion, I prevailed on him to come with me to see a friend who was in need. The story goes like this:

Mary and I went to a party for one of her friends. We were not particularly interested in staying too long, since we felt that we had already given proper attention to the main celebrant. As it happened, we didn't leave quite soon enough, because the feature entertainer was brought in to display her wares. As we left, we couldn't help but wonder why we had even fallen into such a situation. Soon we realized that there was some advantage to this visit, after all. At the party we had learned from a former boss of Mary that his friend (and, coincidentally, my friend) John Kovalcheck was ill with cancer. With this information, I knew that I should pay John a visit, especially since I hadn't seen him in several years. Because John lived next door to Bob Mihalco, we stopped in at Bob's to get more information about John. It was here that we learned that John hadn't been to church in twenty years. I thought it appropriate that I go next door and give John a scapular to wear.

John and his wife, Corey, met me at the door and received me warmly. I got right down to business, reached over, and hung a scapular around his neck before he knew what hit him. Then I asked John if he'd like to go back to church. I got a quick negative reply—there was no success with that question. Well then, I thought, maybe John would like to see a priest. No, no, that didn't work either. "John," I said, "I understand from Bob that you have read my book, *Our Guide*. In there, I speak of Father Ambrosi. Do you remember him?" Oh yes, John replied. It was rather obvious that John was impressed with the little information that I had written about Father, so I used this ploy to proceed further and ask, "Would you see him?" "Yeah—I'd see *him*," John said.

The next thing to do was to take Father Ambrosi over to see John. I was determined that this was not going to be just a plain old visit, so I presented Father to John at the doorway and left abruptly. Maybe an hour or so later I went back, and Father was ready to leave. Not only had he had a nice visit, but he also had heard John's confession.

Two weeks later, John died of pancreatic cancer. At the funeral services, I went up to the first pew to offer condolences to Corey. She couldn't control herself—she jumped forward, hugged me, and said, "Francis, you brought us back to church!"

Chapter Eleven

Wonderful Memories

*I*n 1990, Mary and I visited Europe again. This time we stayed for about seventeen days and visited Ireland only. We pursued our plan of renting a car and driving all over the island, giving particular attention to the places of historic interest in the life of Malachy Naughten, Mary's father. He had been born in Athlone in 1894 and was quite a remarkable Catholic man. He was an outstanding example to all who had the good fortune to know him. I felt that I was never able to adequately express my true feelings to him when I told him on numerous occasions that he was my model. He and Mary Naughten (senior) were to me the ideal in-laws. To us, they were Dad and Mom. They moved from Claremont up to Castro Valley in the 1970s. Sometime after Mom died in 1980, Dad accepted our invitation to live with us in Alta Loma. The few years that he spent here were a period of spiritual enlightenment. Because we lived with him, I got to know him in a way that could not have been done otherwise. What a blessing!

A MEMORABLE ARCHBISHOP

Here is a recounting of my experiences with the stalwart Joseph Francis Rummel, archbishop of New Orleans, under whom I served on many occasions.

I was an altar boy at the St. Louis Cathedral Church in New Orleans for many years, having begun to serve when I was about six years of age. In early 1935, when I was ten, I attended the funeral Mass of Archbishop Shaw and saw him being buried under the flooring in the sanctuary in front of the main altar in the St. Louis Cathedral.

On numerous previous occasions I had attended the Masses over which the Archbishop presided. In this manner, I became acquainted with the high office of Archbishop.

Soon thereafter, in April or May, we received word that our new Archbishop was to be Joseph Francis Rummel, who was then the Bishop of Omaha.

For at least the next six years, I served many High Masses that Archbishop Rummel celebrated. This was his church, the Cathedral Church of the Archdiocese. He often came and celebrated the ten o'clock High Mass, and when he wasn't actually present, it would not be uncommon for us to have a pastoral letter from him to be read at all of the Masses. Frequently, I was assigned to carry either the crosier or the miter for him. In this capacity, I sat by his feet at his throne as he preached. In fact, my position was so close to him that I was struck frequently by his flowing cape as he gestured with his arms during his sermons. I witnessed an intense, unwavering theologian, vociferously guiding his archdiocese in moral principles and preaching against communism, abortion, and racism. The first two of these subjects were totally foreign to me, distant mysteries. Racism, however, was something that I could understand because I had witnessed it. He even excommunicated a man in one of the parishes for his racist agenda. Fortunately, this event was ameliorated at a later date.

At this early stage in my life, I thought this Archbishop was a very, very good man, but his personality intimidated me; he was a rigid German. Yet because of his inherent holiness and evangelical fervor, I deeply admired him. He impressed me profoundly.

I served in World War II and later in the Korean War, and then moved permanently to California. The events of my youth faded into the past and took their place somewhere way back in the recesses of my memory.

Many years later, on November 1, 1964, I dreamed of Archbishop Rummel's death and in this same dream witnessed his burial under the sanctuary floor of the St. Louis Cathedral. Upon awakening, I wondered if this Archbishop, whom I had so admired, might now be sick.

One week later, on November 8, 1964, Archbishop Rummel died and was buried exactly as I had seen in my dream. I was not able to attend the funeral in New Orleans because I was in California, but the account that I read in the paper precisely verified the details that I had seen in my dream.

All of the bishops who were buried in the sanctuary have a memorial plaque in their honor. They are situated side by side by the main altar. Because I had observed his episcopate so closely and admired

St. Louis Cathedral

him so intensely, I am deeply elated whenever I read the plaque dedicated to Archbishop Rummel on the wall of the Cathedral, just near the Altar of the Blessed Sacrament—by the priedieu that the Pope used during his recent visit. This plaque shouts out a message ever so strongly.

After entering the Church and going up the main aisle, go to the steps of the main altar, turn left, and walk until you hit the church wall. There, you will see—most appropriate, most precise, absolutely true—the words on this plaque, which read as follows:

The Most Reverend
Joseph Francis Rummel
Ninth Archbishop of New Orleans
1935-1964
Born 14 October 1876 Ordained 24 May 1902.
Consecrated Bishop of Omaha 29 May 1928.
Installed as Archbishop of New Orleans and
Invested with Pallium
16 May 1935.
Appointed Assistant at Pontifical Throne
27 February 1949.
Retired 24 May 1962.
Died 8 November 1964.

Strong man of God, intrepid champion of human dignity. Kind loving father of the poor. True shepherd in Christ. Rock like in loyalty to God and Church. His clergy, religious and laity beg the Heavenly Father to grant him forever rest, light and peace.

The text below is taken from the booklet "The Basilica on Jackson Square" by Leonard V. Huber and Samuel Wilson, Jr.:

Joseph Francis Rummel was born in Baden, Germany, on October 14, 1876, but came with his parents to the United States when a young child. After study at St. Mary's College, North East, Pennsylvania, at St. Anselm's College in Manchester, New Hampshire, and St. Joseph's Seminary at Dunwoodie, New York, he went to Rome, where, after studying at the North

Vestigia

American College, he received his doctorate in theology and was ordained in 1902. On his return to the United States, he served in several churches in New York. In 1928 he was appointed Bishop of Omaha, where he served until his appointment as Archbishop of New Orleans. On May 15, 1935, he took possession of his See.

Thus began a career which was to span nearly three decades of service in the Crescent City. During this period, the city and state emerged from the Great Depression into a period of unprecedented economic progress.

Archbishop Rummel met the challenge by completely reorganizing the work of the church to meet the growth of Catholicity in this region. He created many new parishes, enlarged seminaries, and developed religious, educational, and charitable institutions. As promoter and host of the Eighth National Eucharistic Congress held in New Orleans in 1938 and for his courageous efforts in the great social changes which took place in the 1950s and 1960s, he achieved national fame. To him fell the honor in April, 1960, of welcoming at the Cathedral President Charles De Gaulle of France. During his regime, the St. Louis Cathedral received major repairs, air-conditioning, a new organ, structural reinforcement, water-proofing, and flood lighting.

After a full life, Archbishop Rummel passed away on November 8, 1964, at the age of 88. His remains, after solemn services at the Cathedral, were entombed under the sanctuary, the eighth Ordinary to lie in this hallowed spot.

•••••••••••••••••••••••••••••••••••••••

If it were not for our move to Alta Loma in 1973, we never would have had the opportunity of having visitors from various religious communities. Since we are able to provide overnight accommodations most of the time, we are fortunate to have numerous nuns and priests spend time with us. Our home has been a gift to us from God, and we know it. We enjoy maintaining it.

Here is an article that I wrote at the request of a local newspaper. It was published in the *Grapevine Press*:

September 27, 1998

In early 1973, a home on Hellman Avenue in Alta Loma offered the potential for much-needed space for my family. So we seized the opportunity to move from La Verne.

Time went by, Alta Loma grew, and traffic increased. It now became evident that our driveway on Hellman Avenue was a terrible hazard. When our car would reach the end of the driveway and nose out into the street, it was difficult for the driver to see oncoming traffic from the North due to the ubiquitous eucalyptus trees which lined the curb and obstructed the view.

Eight huge trees (as broad as four feet in diameter) lined the front of my property, and several others occupied my neighbor's land to the North. Seven of these trees were my nemesis—six of them being mine and one belonged to my neighbor. Any effort that I made to have these trees removed for the sake of safety was met with failure.

During the last week in December of 1996, I was on our front driveway awaiting the mail truck, and I was looking up at the Eucalyptus trees. I said, "Lord, please take these trees. I know it is like asking You to move a mountain, but You could do it."

On January 7, 1997 we had a severe windstorm with winds about 100 mph. As a result, at about 2 A.M., six Eucalyptus trees in a row across the front of our property were blown down. For the most part, they were one on top of the other, lying in a North-South line across our driveway and piled to a height of about 15 feet so that we could not see our neighbor's house across the street. Additionally, another tree, close by to the North and on the adjacent property, was blown down so that seven trees in all were felled. These were the seven offending trees which I had asked to be removed.

·······································

After pondering this tremendous event, I realize that there is another significant point to be made: *no other trees on our block were blown down by this wind!*

Vestigia

I could never say enough in praise of our dear friend Father Snoj. When the Nazis seized his native Slovenia, he was saying Mass in the National Shrine in Brezje. As the Germans entered one door, he escaped through another. Upon Father Snoj's departure, on the feast of Saint Stanislaus, there were to be no more Masses in this basilica for the duration of the war.

Later, Father Snoj fled from the Communists; again it was on the feast of Saint Stanislaus. He soon found himself in Italy in a camp for displaced persons outside of Rome, where he served for four years. Always a priest, he put every bit of his energy into the service of his fellow refugees. Because he had lost all of his priestly attire, he was unrecognizable in army fatigues as he stood before Pope Pius XII with a contingent of other priests. When the Pope faced Father Snoj, he asked, "Are you a priest?" "Yes, I am," Father replied. After three identical inquiries, the Pope became convinced of Father Snoj's identity. In 1948, Father came to Southern California and diligently learned English. He served in several different parishes in both the San Diego and the San Bernardino dioceses.

Father Snoj was such an integral part of our life for so long that many events in his life come to mind from time to time. Sometimes a bird will remind me of the relationship that Father had with them. When he told me that he was followed on foot by a bird as he traversed back and forth in his courtyard while he was reading his breviary, I surely did not discount the possibility. This mutual acquaintance that he had, however, became vivid when I was speaking to him one day in front of his house. We stood face to face with about two feet of space between us as a bird sat high up on the eave, peering at him. Soon he left his perch and swooped down; he flew between us at chest height as if to make certain that we were aware of his presence.

Mary and I kept in close touch with him when he moved from Etiwanda back to Slovenia. It had previously been a part of Yugoslavia, but now it had its independence.

Mary's loyalty was of such a nature that she actually wrote seventy-five letters to Father over a period of two and a half years. We tried to comply with his few simple requests. After living there for about two years, Father Snoj told us in one of our phone conversations that there was one more request that he would like fulfilled before he died. He wanted us to visit him in his native land. He even offered to fund our trip, but, of course, that wasn't necessary. When we decided to make the trip, it was a blessing to be provided with a place to stay in his rectory for five days in February of 1997. Thus, mainly because of Father's request, we decided to make another pilgrimage to Europe, and it was crowned with extraordinary success. John and Jean Leach also made this trip, and they, too, were welcomed at the rectory in Ljubljana, Slovenia.

Father David Sereno, a longtime friend of ours, played a significant role in our pilgrimage. He had been studying at the Gregorian University in Rome for five years and during that time had received his Masters degree in Canon Law. Now he was continuing his studies in Rome and was on the brink of his doctorate. We were very happy to be able to provide a place in our home that could lend a peaceful setting for him to prepare his dissertation. I edited the first ninety pages of this work and realized my limitation. Then, through Mary's recommendation, we elicited the help of Margaret Coates to completely edit the document. Margaret has a PhD in English from Harvard, and I was happy to concede this task in her favor.

In February, Father David was to return to Rome to await scheduling for a defense of his thesis. He mentioned to me that he was requesting the privilege of saying Mass at the tomb of Saint Peter and was also requesting to concelebrate Mass with the Holy Father. When I expressed interest in going to Rome, he said that he would be happy to try to include us with him if his two requests were granted. That is what finally convinced me that we should go on this trip to Europe. Father Snoj wanted us to go, Father David wanted us to go, and also at this time, Mother Lillian Diaz, our friend in Tecate, Mexico, would be in Rome. What other reasons must we need to make our decision?

One can never spend enough time in Rome. This was my second visit, and it was the third for Mary. We visited all of the churches that we had intended to see, thoroughly enjoying our visit to Saint Clement's to relive the lives of Saints Cyril and Methodius. We appreciated Father Snoj's suggestion for this church visit.

As our days in Rome came closer and closer to an end, I was disappointed because Father David had not received a reply to his request to concelebrate with the Holy Father. We were very pleased, though, to be with Father David at his Mass at the tomb of St. Peter. This wish was granted, and for us it was memorable.

Vestigia

At last, it was Friday afternoon, and Mary and I were scheduled to leave for home the next day. The other people that we were with, however, were not leaving until the following Monday. Why don't we stay two more days also? I thought. Maybe that would allow enough time for word of a papal visit to come through. Therefore, Mary and I journeyed to downtown Rome to the airline ticket office to extend our stay until Monday at a cost of $150 each. We prayed that if it be God's will, we would soon get word from the Vatican to visit the Pope. On several occasions, we had had the privilege of seeing the Holy Father high up in his window when we were down in Saint Peter's Square. We even had seen him at his general audience when we were there along with tens of thousands. Also, we had seen the Holy Father celebrate Mass at a beatification ceremony in 1979. At that time we were in the third row of pews in Saint Peter's. But I wanted something different now. I knew that Father David had asked to be allowed to concelebrate Mass with the Pope, and if we were to be with him for that Mass, we surely would be allowed to meet him personally. That's what I hoped for, and that's what I prayed for.

Friday passed, Saturday passed, and when we hadn't heard anything by Sunday morning, we packed our things and went back to Saint Peter's for Mass and toured Rome for the last time. Once back at the hotel, we prepared for the next day's departure.

At about four in the afternoon we received a beautiful phone call. Whoever phoned said that we were to be at the Bronze Door of the Vatican at 6:30. Immediately, I assumed that they meant 6:30 in the morning for a concelebrated Mass; therefore, I unpacked my bag and went to bed for a nap. It wasn't long before we received another call from Joe Senteno, one of our friends, asking how soon would we be going to the Vatican. He insisted that we were supposed to go there that very day at 6:30. Fortunately, we were able to confirm through a priest friend that we were to meet at 6:30 that evening at the Bronze Door. We flew across the city of Rome by cab and arrived with about twenty minutes to spare. There we met with Father David, who again confirmed that we would have an audience with the Pope that very evening. Our prayers had been answered!

We were frisked by the Italian police and then approved by the Swiss Guards, brought in through the Bronze Door, and escorted up sixty-seven marble steps. We then boarded an elevator to ascend four more flights up to what I assume was the papal apartment.

About two hundred fifty of us were assembled in a very large parlor, each of the groups of pilgrims spread out about two-deep against the walls. Finally, after about twenty minutes, the Holy Father came into the room and slowly made his way around the room, stopping in front of each group and even stopping to talk to each individual who wished to speak to him.

In about forty-five minutes, the Pope arrived at our group of about 13, and it was awesome! It is impossible to describe the feeling that one gets in the presence of the Holy Father. I remember reading about the lives of various saints (e.g. Saint Theresa and Saint Francis of Assisi) who were privileged to have an audience with the Pope. I never could understand how they were able to achieve this, because I knew that one could not just decide "I'm going to see the Pope." Yet, I knew that it sometimes happened; therefore, it may happen someday for me. When my opportunity came, and I looked to my right, there he was—the Holy Father himself—about ten feet away, walking directly toward Mary and me. He looked us right in the eye, and when he reached us, we each fell to our knees and kissed his hand. I felt his ring and pondered its significance. Even though I have always made it a point to kiss the ring of a bishop, I don't think I kissed the Holy Father's ring. Instead, I kissed his hand repeatedly. Here we were, unencumbered, face to face with the Holy Father himself!

Mary held the Holy Father's left hand, kissed it, and told him, "Truly you are Peter! Thank you." After a couple of more kisses and expressions of love to him, it was my turn.

When I held the right hand of the Holy Father, I kissed it three times in between my words to him. I said, "Holy Father, we love you, Holy Father we support you." I placed a written list of names which Mary had prepared in his hand and gave him a set of Little Feet (representing the unborn babies) as well. His response to us was, "Americanos!" When I asked him to bless the religious articles that were in my bag, the priest at his side said that he had already done so. It was a tremendous thrill to be able to hold his right hand while Mary held his left and there was no one crowding us while we took our time and spoke directly to him. He waited patiently for us to finish. I hated to let him go. As I held his hand, I thought, here is the hand that has blessed so many people and this ring of his, the Fisherman's Ring, I am actually feeling it around his finger. It took us a long time afterward to

Vestigia

adjust to the ordinary life, because now we were descending from the clouds.

It was a few weeks later, after we had left Rome, that Father David received his doctorate in Canon Law, *summa cum laude* from the Pontificia Università Gregoriana. The subject of his dissertation was "Whether the Norm Expressed in canon 1103 is of Natural Law or of Positive Church Law." This text proudly adorns our bookshelf.

In succeeding months, we made our usual trips up to Napa, California, and we made frequent other trips. Mostly we traveled to Tecate, Mexico, but we also visited my brother Mike in San Antonio and Muriel in New Orleans. Generally, Mary and I went to New Orleans about once each year. In fact, during the course of our marriage, Mary had traveled to New Orleans about 32 times when I stopped counting the trips a couple of years ago. Because of our loved ones, New Orleans is very important to us. And we enjoy the city too, especially the wonderful food.

It is always good to find new places for seafood in the New Orleans area. On one of our trips across the lake to Lacombe, we went to Farrell's restaurant on the advice of one of the Sisters at Muriel's house. I had previously been to Sal and Judy's down the road on Highway 190, but never had I been to Farrell's. Their menu was exciting, and their oysters were not disappointing. While we were eating, I looked over my shoulder just to get a view of the restaurant. A lot of memorabilia was on display to capture your interest as you waited for your food. There, on a piano, I saw a picture that looked familiar; it was the Jesuit High School Band, and I was clearly distinguishable in the clarinet section. The picture probably had been taken in 1938. When I inquired from the management how they had obtained the picture, I got another lesson in humility. They had acquired the photo in a garage sale!

In 1997, I sold the land that I had held in Lacombe for forty-eight years. At that time, my sister Mary again became my "agent" when she transacted this sale. Among other things, there was a complicated title problem that had to be dealt with. It would have been very difficult for me to handle it from my home in California, and her assistance was absolutely invaluable. Now, since Papa and Mama Dueñas were deceased and I no longer owned any property there, I consider myself finally separated from an era that was monumental in my life. I remember the nostalgia that I used to feel any time I saw the beautiful twin pine that adorned the lawn. It had special significance to me, because it was under this tree that I studied for my college comprehensive exams.

As my years moved on, I became more and more involved in one aspect of the Eucharistic ministry, that of visiting the homebound parishioners. So often, in my mind, I could envision myself or other dear ones and even parishioners unknown to me, who were not able to attend Mass. Who would provide home visitation with the Blessed Sacrament to these people if others who were able did not step forward and volunteer to do so? I am profoundly thankful for the privilege that is granted to us in this ministry.

We have been dedicated to the aid of the unfortunate victims of abortion for many years, but I have not been accepted by callers on our Pregnancy Counseling Center hotline. Primarily, they want to speak to a woman. Occasionally they will tolerate me; therefore, I am only marginally successful. I do try, however, to lend aid to Mary, whose devotion to this cause knows no limit.

Now, I have become a grandfather, like the one who carried a lantern or the other one who played cylindrical phonograph records. My children have grown and positioned themselves in society. I am proud of their adherence to the Faith and their courage in the face of adversity. They have brought terrific grandchildren into my life. I may get tired, but I never tire of them.

In that group, I place Diana Downard, whom we have adopted in principle. She and her mother, Patricia, stayed with us for a few years and have become an integral part of our family. I continue to marvel at Diana's industrious nature. She is my "Cariño," and *we* speak Spanish together. I am "Papa" to all my grandchildren, and I like to think that maybe someday they will be better people because of something that I taught them or did for them. The satisfaction that comes to a grandparent can only be experienced by one who is also a grandparent.

Among the grandchildren, the ones that became the most present were Vincent and Gabriel, since they live with us. Because I have come to know them so well, I can say that they are an absolute delight! They give evidence of the remarkable job that Linda is doing with them.

Frequently I remind Ann and Bart of their tremendous achievement in raising the twins, Victor and Tavish. Their exuberance and affection reflect the loving nature of their parents. Then there is A. Francis Sturdivant, as I call him, who is called by everyone else

Alan F. Sturdivant. There is absolutely some partiality in my choice of names.

I wish we had the opportunity to visit Gail and Steve more often, but with the trips that we do make, I get to see Brian, Scott, and Maureen as they grow up. I learn from each of them. They excel in graciousness whenever we are able to share with them. They review their projects with me, and I enjoy giving them my approval.

We were able to attend Amy's wedding to Jeff Thomas in Palo Alto in 1999. This was the little girl to whom I used to read. She loved to hear about *Mister Brown's Grocery Store*. I was very pleased to see how Beth and Pamela are maturing. They both were somewhat shy previously. I remember Beth one time years ago telling me that her younger sister, Pamela, was shy. I doubted whether Beth knew what the word "shy" meant, so I asked her. She gave me as cute a reply as you can imagine: "Shy means—shy means—shy means *very shy*!

As parents with four children in school, Dan and Cruz are kept quite busy, but thankfully we are able to see Serena, Michelle, Rachel, and Marion frequently. It is always so interesting for me to see their continuing progress. They have taken my place in the aircraft industry, because they visit planes whenever the opportunity presents itself. Now, for the most part, instead of my visiting the historic aircraft, they do it for me.

I am thankful to my parents for all that they have given to me, and I know that Marion and Mary have been my special blessings. When I review my life, I feel an overpowering need to express thanksgiving to Almighty God for His many gifts—absolutely too numerous to explain.

My brothers and sisters are very close to me, and I hope that they know how much they mean to me. I try to visit them often and would like to see them even more.

There are so many memories that come to mind when I think of each of my siblings. When Maxine was missioned to Mayaguez, Puerto Rico, it seemed so very far away. Whenever she flew into town, we'd meet her at the airport, or when she came by ship, we went to the American Sugar Refinery where she docked. It is so very long ago that I remember Maxine going to La Salle, Illinois; I remember that city because it was famous for its clocks. Then at different times there was Kansas City and Utah and Saragossa, Texas, and Our Lady of Talpa here in California. When Maxine was at Saint Patrick's School on

Clementina Street in San Francisco, Marion and I visited her when we had Mr. and Mrs. Dueñas with us. It was an appropriate time to bring Papa there, because with the little help that I gave him, we were able to fix the window sashes in one of the classrooms for Maxine.

Because of our location near Gertrude when she was at Maryvale, we could spend time with her. Particularly, however, I remember the time long ago when she was in Long Beach, Mississippi, along with Sister Elizabeth. Daddy and Mother took me there with them, and we had delicious creamed cauliflower—the first time for me. We were also able to visit her in Austin.

Of course, I remember Muriel on Emerson Avenue in Saint Mary's Home and the RCO (Roman Catholic Orphanage) in San Francisco, as I previously mentioned. There was another mission that she had in Los Altos, California, and an occurrence there distressed me: one of her young girls—I believe she was twelve—kicked her in the chest. Thank God there were no resultant problems. Since Muriel spent most of her time in New Orleans and that was a favorite place for us to visit, it is natural, then, that we saw her and Mary (who lived in Algiers or Hammond) most frequently.

One situation is very memorable for me regarding the Daughters of Charity. It was in 1944, when I arrived in San Francisco for the first time. I went to one of their convents and rang the bell. I had never been there before, and I had never told them that I was coming. When the door swung open, a Sister appeared and I was greeted with, "Come in, Francis."

I have three big sisters, but it surely is nice having a little sister. I think of all the little things that Mary does. How sad I was when we had to call off our dinner with her in October of 1999 when my Mary got sick. I'll never know all of the trouble she went to preparing a meal of my choice for us and our friends. Then, too, at an earlier date when we visited with her and Eddie for a couple of days, she had rented a comfortable recliner chair just for me. She sends me interesting things in the mail and keeps in touch with me by phone; I like that. My mind drifts through the years, and I recall how helpful Mary was to Marion during the time I was overseas. Without her assistance, they would not have been able to travel to St. Louis to visit Muriel. I wish I could have been at Mary's graduation when she got her degree in history with honors. I was very proud of her.

Vestigia

I am so thankful that we are able to see Mike fairly often. For the beginning of the New Millennium, we were able to visit him in San Antonio and join with the congregation in prayer on this auspicious occasion. I thank God for the graces He has given to many people through Mike's ministry as a priest.

On May 27, 1979, Joe died after an illness of several months; he was only 49 years old. Albert died on October 25, 1992 after battling lung cancer, and Louis, the youngest member of the family, died on June 28, 1999. Almost all of my brothers are gone now; Mike is the only one left.

Chapter Twelve

My Mother

God has a special gift for each of us, a gift that is really beyond description because in its essence it lacks all of the self-seeking rewards with which we are so familiar. The gift that He has chosen for us is our mother. I called my mother "Ma." I remember one time when I was about eight years old and was probably in the fourth grade. One of the Teresian Sisters who was my teacher had told the class that we should go to our mother at night and tell her that we are sorry for anything that we had done wrong that day. That night as I whispered this statement into my mother's ear, I could see that she was most pleased. I had touched her heart.

My mother was so special that on May 17, 1950, Archbishop Rummel conferred on her the Regina Matrum award. The citation read in part: "The honoree this year was chosen by a committee of priest-judges who screened a number of nominations submitted by the pastors of the Archdiocese of New Orleans. The selection of Mrs. Levy was made because of her exemplary life as a successful wife, mother, and homemaker and because of her cumulative contributions to community, parochial, and diocesan life."

I cannot imagine the heavenly reward Our Blessed Lord has bestowed on my mother now that she has completed her pilgrimage on earth. She served Him and she served Him well! Her model was Our Blessed Lady; over and over again she taught us to stay close to the Blessed Mother. She had that message firmly in her mind and imparted it to all of us emphatically when she said, "Don't forget to say the Memorare." "Say a Hail Mary." "Say the Rosary." The Holy Rosary was our standard night prayer as the whole family knelt together by the flickering candlelight.

From my early days, Mother had a most powerful influence on my life. She led me continuously in the right direction; she never faltered. Her words are forever embedded in my mind: "*Please* and *thank you* are never out of place." She often said, "Don't ever say anything unkind about anybody. If you can't say something good about them, then don't say anything." I never heard her utter an unkind word about anybody—*never in my life*! In this she was absolutely inflexible. She taught us to laugh, but we could never learn to laugh like she did—when she got the giggles, she couldn't stop and nobody around her could stop. Whenever we showed signs of congestion or flu, it was common practice for her to give us a rub-down with Sloan's Liniment or sometimes Vick's Vaporub. Some occasions required the more drastic treatment of Citrate of Magnesia or the dreaded castor oil. Nutritionally, her intention for us was the daily regimen of cod liver oil. This was not nearly as offensive as the laxatives, and it seemed to keep us supplied with vitamin D.

My mother sometimes used her own vocabulary, which I had thought to be common for all. A tricycle was called a velocipede (from the Latin meaning "rapidly by foot"), and her purse was usually referred to as her pocketbook.

Parking in the French Quarter is at a premium, and parking at the St. Louis Cathedral Church in the heart of the French Quarter is not allowed. There were two exceptions, however: the Archbishop and my mother.

Everything in Mother's life was centered around her faith. The Sacraments were of the utmost importance, and she received them very frequently. She never shirked her duty, and in a large household, this meant working from early morning until late at night. Then she would go to sleep, utterly exhausted.

I loved to hear Mother recount the vision that she received in her last years. She spoke of it factually but never ostentatiously. She died a mere eleven days shy of her ninety-fourth birthday, surrounded by her children. Then it was that God claimed back His precious gift—a gift He had given to us for a time.

At the funeral parlor, I stood at her casket beside Albert and Archbishop Philip Hannan. It made me feel so happy to see this wonderful archbishop pay tribute to my mother. Later I reflected on the fact that here was the man who, twenty-five years earlier, had been chosen to give the eulogy at President Kennedy's funeral in Washington; now he voluntarily honored my mother and paid homage to my brother Mike by his presence.

When we gathered for her funeral, it was most fitting that her childlike devotion to Our Lady be manifested through the many school

Vestigia

children who came to give tribute to her at the celebration of the Holy Mass. Mike offered the Mass and selected the hymns; when he spoke, Mike gave such tender acclamation to our Mother. The "Memorare" was sung at the beginning of Mass because it was Mother's favorite prayer. At the final hymn, "Hail Mary, Gentle Woman," it was as though Mother were giving a final tribute to the Blessed Virgin Mary through the voices of the children.

Chapter Thirteen

The Greatest Gift

The Gift of the Holy Eucharist is our most precious possession, because it is the very essence of God Himself. He is there, but He is hidden. He wants us to search for Him as He teaches us in Psalm 63:

Oh God, you are my God;
I shall seek you tirelessly.
I long for you, I thirst for you,
Body and soul, as
Parched and desert land without water.

Such am I as I gaze toward you
In your sanctuary,
Longing to see your power and your glory.
For your good pleasure is more precious than life.

My lips shall praise you.
Thus will I bless you
My whole life long. In your name,
I will lift up my hands in prayer.

I shall be filled with happiness and gladness;
With joyful lips my mouth shall praise you.
I shall be mindful of you
As I lay me down to sleep.

Through the hours of the night
I will remember you,
For you have become my helper.
In the shadow of your wings I will rejoice.

My soul clings fast to you;
Your right hand defends me.
Those who seek my life maliciously
Shall meet with death;

They shall be delivered to the sword.
They shall be the prey of wild beasts.
But the king shall rejoice in God;
Everyone who worships Him shall be victorious;

But the mouth of those
Who speak evil shall be stopped.

It wasn't until Marion suggested daily reception of the Holy Eucharist that I began to get a glimmer of this wisdom. Presently, Mary and I are blessed with this wonderful opportunity. I never prayed for this gift; I never knew enough to do so. Possibly, then, Almighty God heard a prayer for some other intention but granted this one instead.

When speaking about our faith to non-Catholics, I like to use their own Bible and resort to John, Chapter 6 as the most profound message in Scripture. When we read these verses, I challenge them: "Can we walk away as many of the disciples did?" I feel that this is the best way to comply with the mandate given to all of us in the last two verses of Matthew.

In my daily prayers, I never neglect the Psalms, but for a long time I let a big one get away. I didn't get acquainted with Psalm 139 until my brother Mike emphasized its importance and its beauty to me. I wonder if this is the "hounding" that was heard by Francis Thompson.

Chapter Fourteen

Our Lady

I cannot overestimate the assistance that I have received from the Blessed Mother throughout the years. Father Aloysius and many other priests and Sisters have taught me to go to her for help. But no one has imparted that message more firmly in my mind than my own mother. As I grew up, there were some things that my mother said daily, and her recommendation to go to Our Lady was one of them. I know that Albert profited from her advice, as well, because I distinctly remember his reference to Our Lady many times. He called her "The Lady," and each time that he said this, he smiled to me and spoke in a reverential tone. I know that it was his prayerful request to her that brought him out of his German prison camp. I try to remember my debt of gratitude for her intercessory help by saying her Little Office every day. If I remember my own mother—which I do—then it's easy to remember Our Lady, because they are so much alike.

Sometimes a particular place will inspire us; sometimes it is special people who lift up our spirits. When I think of a place that is inspirational, I might dwell on the Shrine of Our Lady of Lourdes in France, with its candlelight procession and the Benediction at the healing of the sick or of one of the magnificent churches in Rome. When I think of an individual, I might think of Father Aloysius or Father Ambrosi, who were holy priests, or perhaps my dear friend Jim Buehner, who is an example to all who know him; his staunch, unwavering faith, exhibited in his writings, is a beacon to all. However, when I couple together in my mind the image that reflects both elements—people and place—I come to the scene that Mary and I witnessed in Mexico City in December of 1996. Many groups of pilgrims journeyed up the center section of the street in native costume while singing hymns and chanting prayers. These groups had come from distant cities on this long trek to pay homage to the Virgin of Guadalupe. Others showed their individual devotion and loyalty by their slow forward march on their knees up the street toward the Shrine. Upon their arrival, they continued in this posture up the aisle of the church to the altar rail. This demonstration of prayer to the "Patroness of the Americas" is awesome. Whenever we feel less inclined to exert ourselves and move out of our lassitude, it is uplifting and invigorating to reflect on these scenes.

Chapter Fifteen

Afterthoughts

I often recall the time that I spent on active duty in the navy and relive my many encounters with rough weather. At the onset of such a challenge, when I first went to sea, I prayed that I would not get seasick. I endured five fearsome typhoons (a typhoon is the name for a hurricane occurring in the northwestern Pacific Ocean). During these storms, the ship is tossed about like a shoe box on the water, then comes crashing down and shudders and groans and creaks—you think its going to be torn apart. After it gets twisted and pounded for hours, you become convinced that it is absolutely impossible for this thing to stay together, that it just can't make it. During each storm, I prayed with all my heart. I was afraid of the storm above and afraid of the fury of the sea below. Would I ever see land again? On each occasion, the Lord answered my prayers as I had requested; the storms abated and calm seas prevailed. I realize, too, that I would not have been faced with these storms had I not been protected on many other occasions while in battle. I had prayed, and many others had prayed, too. Never once did I get seasick. Not even those typhoons upset me. Yet there were so many men around me who were violently seasick. The sickness situation was so repetitive that I always knew who would suffer. Some men, however, were not so consistent. They would fall prey to the motion only at certain times. I was continually amazed and continually thankful that I was forever free of this ailment.

There was a specific detail connected with one of the typhoons that we experienced. As we were leaving a harbor with many other ships—all anxious to put to sea as the safest refuge at a time like this—we were bouncing around like a toy in a bathtub. At the same time, the cruiser USS *Salt Lake City* (CL25) was underway nearby, moving swiftly through the water. Many men of her crew were topside, looking at the sight that we presented in the monstrous waves. Their ship was sleek, and its pointed bow knifed the water, whereas our blunt prow presented a colliding wall to the oncoming sea. Just as we cleared the entrance to the harbor, a swell smashed into us; we shuddered and reared upward, but the cruiser dove under the rushing sea, which swept heavily over her deck. A crew member who was busy watching our ship was abruptly swept overboard! It is very difficult and sometimes impossible to recover a man overboard because the inertia of the moving vessel swiftly carries it ahead while the hapless victim struggles in an enormous sea that rapidly dwarfs his image. A small bobbing head soon vanishes from sight. Standard emergency procedure for the officer who is conning the ship is to stop the engines and shift the rudder over immediately to the side of the tragedy. This action kicks the stern away from the victim, getting him out of the way of the propellers. Of course, immediate signals are passed on to the vessels astern to provide clearance and begin the search. Even in this tumultuous sea, everything must have worked well in this rescue procedure, for the sailor was soon lifted from the sea. Many months later, when the U.S. was conducting special testing at the Bikini Atoll, an atomic bomb was dropped on many outmoded naval vessels targeted there. The USS *Salt Lake City* was one of the doomed ships that were sent to the bottom by the blast.

The beauty and majesty of the open sea is matchless. Flying fish and porpoises provide company cruising alongside. They give a feeling of partnership in this vast ocean. The effortless flight of the albatross far away from land offers hope for our return to a stable and friendly shore. The display of nature, particularly at sunset, is made manifest to those who are present to behold it. Bold and pastel hues vie for attention, as the scene is only momentary. Incremental panoramas dazzle the eye. Away from the noise and lights of civilization, the hand of the Artist is displayed in all of its grandeur. As the sun sinks below the horizon, it is as though the water would come to a boil by the immersion. Little by little the sky begins to darken, and the steady, bright radiance of the planets appear, each competing for attention. When the glow of twilight has totally disappeared, the grip of night is at hand. The twinkle of a vast multitude of stars in a blackened sky is a reminder of the trillions of grains of sand along the beach—for we are told that the number of stars is more numerous than the grains of sand on the seashore. Is it really true that each of these millions of stars is identified, or is it possible that maybe I can see some that no one else has seen? So many shooting stars sweep across the sky, never again to shine, yet how few are present to witness this one burst of life, resplendent in its fiery plunge into the atmosphere. Even the sea beneath competes for attention as the glow of plankton disturbed by the passage of a ship illuminates the waterline. Soon, a full, brilliant moon illuminates the sky and forces the lesser lights to hide as it rises and assumes dominance to become the sun of the night, casting a silvery sheen on a sea that once was black. To travel in a convoy of "darkened ships," anxious to achieve safety from detection by the enemy, is to travel in the theater of the perfect planetarium. If this is the Heavens, if this is where God is, then I, too, want to be here. As the ship rises and falls on a gentle rolling sea and a soft breeze wafts through the rigging, you wonder: can this be the same ocean that opened up its jaws in an attempt to devour me? Is this breeze the same wind that blew with anger, forcing me to hold fast to a stanchion lest I be blown away? If this wind and this sea are really the same culprits, I feel inclined to forgive them, because they seem to be making that entreaty. Yet I am untrusting; I've seen this scenario before, and I've witnessed this fickle sea. Yet, both aspects of this environment are creations in perfect compliance with the laws of its Master. I never could have dreamed of the magnificence of the sea when I stood on the dock of the Mississippi and observed the vessels tied to their mooring, bobbing up and down on a friendly river. They appeared to be incapable of disturbance. Even amidst the splendor of the sea, unique beyond words, I am called by my own nature to seek that environment for which I was made. For I am ever mindful of the forces at sea, which, although they may lie dormant, are always lurking with the possibility of terror. I must resort to Latin for an adequate expression: I need *terra firma* (solid ground); the more "firma," the less "terror."

••••••••••••••••••••••••••••••••••••••

The US LST Association, of which I am a member, seeks to hold together the dwindling group of survivors of this branch of the Amphibious Service. They publish a bi-monthly periodical of activities and nostalgic memories. Whenever I review these pages, it doesn't take long to visualize myself, once again, aboard one of the vessels that is underway. In the LST Association, I am a member with triple credentials: LST-712, LST-683, and LST-1101.

Francis X. Levy

••

On a particular morning in 1945, when all of New York City was engulfed in fog, a Mitchell B25 Bomber was heading for a nearby airport, but the pilot lost his bearings as he attempted to cross Manhattan. Suddenly, a tall building appeared directly ahead; in an attempt to avoid a collision, he banked away but was unsuccessful. He crashed into the north side of the Empire State Building, disabling elevators and spreading fires. The 79th floor of the structure was hardest hit. Thirteen people were killed, including the three who were aboard the plane.

Even though it was a Saturday, a group of Catholic laymen were meeting on the very floor of the tragedy. Among those who were killed was the national president of the Catholic Evidence Guild. Since my father was the national vice-president at that time, he then rose to the presidency. At the next national assembly, he continued as president when he was then elected to that office.

During this era, Walter Romig's publication, *The American Catholic Who's Who*, included each member of our family in its biographical sketch when it gave note of my father's prominence. The following data is taken verbatim from that publication:

> LEVY. ALBERT ALLEN, lawyer; b. New Orleans, Jan. 11 '93; s. Marx and Gertrude Coralie (Castro) L.; educ. Boys H.S. '10, LL.B. Loyola U., '26; m. Henrietta Catherine Schaeffer, Aug. 14 '16; ch. —Maxine Rose (Sister Maxine, Dau. Of Charity of St. V. de P.), Gertrude Mary (Sister Henrietta, id), Muriel Agnes (Sister Miriam, id), Albert A., Jr., Francis Xavier, Mary Louise, Joseph Anthony, Michael Henry (O.M.I.), Louis Vincent. Since '07 plays music professionally, as side-line and as hobby; ex-pres. Local 174, A.F.M.; internal revenue agt., U.S. Govt., '22 – '44; since in pvt. Law practice. Appointed procurator-advocate of Matrimonial Tribunal, New Orleans Archdiocese, Oct. '55. Mem.: Cath. Evidence Guild (officer N.O. br. Since founded '38, and pres. '45 — ; natl. v.p. '44-45, and pres., '45-46; T.O.S.F. (novice master Portiuncula Frat.; prefect '37-43), Holy Name Soc. (pres., N.O. Metropol. Council, '48-50); K. of C. (ex-trustee). Amateur radio operator (W5FXX). Father died in Jewish faith but kept Cath. Marriage promises; wife given Matrum Regina award, '50. H: 1123 Royal St., New Orleans, 16, La.

Vestigia

••

For the most part, every job that I've had has been challenging. Rarely have I been bored in my employment. This is so important for one who has to go out every day into the marketplace. I feel for those who have not been similarly blessed. I hope that I remember to pray often for them.

••

Interesting stories will forever come to mind, and something that was quite serious at the time can now become a chuckle:

Before Holy Name of Mary Church was erected in La Verne, I used to attend morning Mass at Our Lady of Guadalupe Church, about a mile away. One rainy morning, before entering the church, I met a large, wet dog that was blocking the doorway. I carefully nudged this shaggy dog aside so that I could pass. I was determined to block his entry and not allow his wet fur to get my suit wet. My action prevented this lost animal from coming into the church. Soon after the Mass began, a woman who entered the church was not as successful in preventing this dog's attendance at Mass. After he came in and shook off the water, he could have settled down on the floor to take advantage of the shelter that he had found. Not exactly. He had other ideas. Just as Father Raphael Flammia began to read the Gospel, the dog thought that he should join Father on the altar. He was so happy up there in the middle of the sanctuary that his wagging tail and exuberance became a major distraction that required some action. Immediately, Doctor Paul Cottrell, our dentist, joined me; together we became dogcatchers. It so happened that the dog had positioned himself on a large, oval rug that lay atop the asphalt tile flooring. This floor must have had a nice coating of wax on it, because the rug slid easily every which way as the dog romped about in his further effort to elude us. In our attempt to capture this animal quietly and prevent a disturbance in church, we had instead created a ruckus! Father Raphael continued to read the Gospel as Paul and I pranced around and around with this dog on the sliding rug. When we finally were able to grab him, we carried him into the sacristy and closed the door. Soon, we decided on his fate. Since the window was only a few feet above ground level, we enticed him to depart by that route. He was a nice dog, probably the only one in the neighborhood that had been to Mass that day. And Doctor Cottrell and I smelled like we had been to the same Mass.

••

My favorite feast day is the Annunciation because of its most profound significance. Additionally, for my own private celebration, I hold the feast of the Presentation to be a very special day. On that day I celebrate the anniversary of a great gift that I received through the prayers of Father Aloysius. It was also he who introduced me to the *Little Office of the Blessed Virgin Mary* on August 22, 1962. At that time, this was the feast of the Immaculate Heart of Mary, a feast of great importance to the Claretian Fathers. This gift from Father Aloysius was most gratefully appreciated.

••

Patience is a virtue that I greatly admire. When I fail in my attempt to acquire it, I guess I should use my father's expression that he used to denote exasperation: "*E pluribus unum ciobus cinicum comiatibus sunt swampo*"—a phrase that really doesn't exist. And when he was on a ladder and someone asked him what he was doing, his reply was a humorous "I'm frying eggs." With such a good example, perhaps I will succeed in acquiring this virtue.

Also, I remember that he told us what his grandmother used to say about the house when Uncle Edmund used the attic for weightlifting and Daddy used the downstairs room for his chemistry. Her comment was: "I don't know whether the house is going to cave in from the top or blow up from the bottom." It sounds like she had patience, too.

In these pages, I have attempted to narrate the events that have filled seventy-six years. It would take many more pages to cover everything that I have to say, but I hope that I have covered the most significant events.

I cannot muse over these many years without arriving at a most important fact: *I have been blessed.* Who could ever be able to count his blessings! In every era of my life I see a preponderance of Divine Assistance.

QUOD ERAT FACIENDUM

Chapter Sixteen

Addendum

*F*rom: *Dictionary of American Naval Fighting Ships*, Vol. VI (1976), pp. 263, counties in Arkansas, Illinois, Kansas, Missouri, and Nebraska.

(LST-1101: displacement 1,625 tons, length 328', beam 50', draft 13' speed 12 knots; complement 119 crew; troops 147; armament 8 40mm and 12 20mm guns; class LST-511).

LST-1101 was laid down on 22 November 1944 by the Missouri Valley Bridge and Iron Co., Evansville Ind.; launched on 3 January 1945, sponsored by Mrs. James J. Tolson; placed in reduced commission on 20 January 1945 and taken down the Mississippi and commissioned in full at New Orleans on 26 January 1945. After serving in the Pacific for several months, she left Pearl Harbor in November and continued on to California. In January 1946, she proceeded to Seattle to begin inactivation; and, on 6 June, she was decommissioned and berthed with the Pacific Reserve Fleet.

Ordered activated again in August 1950, as the war in Korea moved into its third month, LST-1101 was recommissioned on 3 November. In December, she arrived at her home port, San Diego. In January 1951, she trained in local waters, and, in February, she sailed west. On 23 March, she arrived at Yokosuka; shifted to Camp McGill to load personnel and vehicles of A Company, 101st Signal Battalion on 1 April, then headed for Inchon. Offloaded on the 8th, she returned to Japan on the 11th and carried cargo between Japanese ports for the remainder of the month. In May, she again delivered men and cargo to Inchon; and, in June, she returned to cargo runs in the Japanese home islands. In July and August, she conducted amphibious exercises, then, in September, she returned to Korea.

On the 10th, LST-1101 embarked Republic of Korea Army troops at P'ohang Dong, transported them to Cheju Do, then, from the 15th to the 28th, conducted shuttle runs between Pusan and the offshore, POW inhabited island of Koje Do. On 29 October, she returned to Japan and, toward the end of November, departed Yokosuka for San Diego.

Arriving on 19 December, LST-1101 conducted local exercises into the spring of 1952. Overhaul followed [and in the month of September, I completed my tour of duty and returned to New Orleans for separation]. After that date, the ship returned to the Pacific for additional duty.

With the return of more peaceful conditions, LST-1101 named Saline County on 1 July 1955, rotated regularly between San Diego-based training exercises and cargo runs and duty with the 7th Fleet in the western Pacific. Ranging from Japan to the Philippines during her 7th Fleet deployments, she covered the west coast and operated in the Hawaiian Islands while with the 1st Fleet. In November 1958, she completed her last western Pacific tour. A year later, she shifted to Alaskan shuttle runs; and, in 1960, she was ordered inactivated.

Saline County was decommissioned on 9 March 1960 and her name was struck from the navy list on 1 November of the same year. Later, she was transferred to Germany, converted to a mine layer, and served the German Navy as Bottrop (N-121) until September 1971 when she was decommissioned and scrapped.

Chapter Seventeen

Lagniappe

On the Occasion of My Eightieth Birthday

A frequent topic for discussion when relatives gather is the family tree. Do we have one? How far back does it go? How comprehensive is it? This, of course, is a conversation that is open-ended in both directions: we never discover the beginning, and the end always lies in the distant future. Yes, there is a family tree, there always is one; but has anyone ever compiled it?

Many years ago, my brother Joe did some valiant work in this regard. In fact, his energy was really superhuman; he spared no effort in his search through libraries, church registries, and official documents to amass an amazing database. At this time, only a fraction of this history has been assembled, and the tree continues to grow. Maybe now is the time to review the situation and give further thought to our position.

If we choose one point, the era of my parents, Albert and Henrietta Levy, and trace backward as far as we can and then proceed from that same point as far forward as possible, we can produce a creditable structure. Whatever can be compiled is always substance for insertion in the family Bible, and certainly it serves to bring about and maintain closer family ties.

With these ideas in mind, I asked my sister Mary Levy Brown to work with me in the development of a genealogy that would be rather broad and definitive. Willingly, she has put herself to the task and provided much foliage for our tree.

In addition, Mary has made several original sketches for insertion in this book so that the generations that we list can share their heritage of origin as well as the family tradition of art. I am indeed indebted to Mary for her contributions.

ALBERT ALLEN LEVY AND
HENRIETTA CATHERINE SCHAEFFER LEVY

(Family Tree of **"Granny" Rosalie "Rose" Ruth** and **Henry Joseph Schaeffer**, parents of **Henrietta Catherine Schaeffer**)

Descendants of Adam Ruth and Catherine Ebisch:

Adam Ruth (1826–1875) from Germany and **Catherine Ebisch** (1827–1893) from France were married May 9, 1848, in New Orleans, LA. They had the following children:

1. Adam   (1849–1892)
2. Catherine   (1850–1935)
3. Nicholas   (1851–1893)
4. Caroline   (1853–??)
5. Elizabeth   (1854–1856)
6. Mary   (1856–1940)
7. George   (1858–1865)
8. William—twin   (1860–1933)
9. Francis "Frank"—twin (1860–1915)
10. Margaretha "Maggie" (1862–1947)
11. "Granny" Rosalie   (1864–1951)
12. Andrew   (1868–1909)
13. James Frederick   (1870–1939)

Descendants of Peter Schaeffer (1811–1903) and Marianne Gossmann (1814–??):

Both were from Germany and were married April 24, 1837, in Frammersbach, Germany. Peter and Marianne had nine children, one of which was **Frank Lawrence** (father of **Henry Joseph "Grandpa" Schaeffer**).

Frank Lawrence (1838–1880) from Germany and **Maria Scherer** (1844–1871) were married in 1859 in St. Mary's Assump-

Vestigia

tion Church, New Orleans, LA. They had four children: Frank, **Henry Joseph**, Julia, and Mary Elizabeth. Frank Lawrence was a retail grocer in New Orleans.

Rosalie "Granny" Ruth (1864–1951) and **Henry Joseph "Grandpa" Schaeffer** (1861–1927) were married in St. Francis Church in New Orleans, LA.

Note: Grandpa Schaeffer had several different occupations during his lifetime, such as delivering ice to groceries and as a laborer in a sugar refinery. He also sold wholesale supplies to groceries. When his facilities burned down without insurance coverage, he was forced out of business.

Their children were:
    1. Agnes "Auntie" Claire   (1885–1971)
        Agnes married James T. Heyden
        Their children:
            1. Oliver
            2. Dorothy

2. Henrietta Catherine,   B (01-14-94) D (01-03-88)

    3. Herbert Andrew   (1901–??)
        Herbert married Vera Martin
        Their children:
            1. Herbert, Jr.
            2. Norma

(Family Tree of **Gertrude Coralie Castro** and **Marx Levy**, parents of **Albert Allen Levy**)

Descendants of Felipe Luis Castro (1836-1901) and Coralie Eliza Blanchard (1848–1927)

Felipe was from Lugo, Spain, and Coralie is of French-Acadian descent. They married in Baton Rouge, LA, in 1863. She was 15 years old, and he was 27.

Their children:
1. David (died as a baby)
2. Dennis
3. Joseph
4. Louis
5. Emile
6. Charles
7. **Gertrude Coralie**
8. Mamie
9. Leonora

Descendants of Herman Levy (1831–1921) and Rosa Zadek (18?? –1920)

Herman and Rosa were from Eastern Europe, most probably Poland. They married in Europe. Herman and Rosa were Orthodox Jews and spoke Yiddish.

Their children:
1. **Marx (1866–1930)**
2. Louis
3. Julius
4. Michael
5. Adolph

Note: Herman Levy tried his hand at several different occupations: he operated side shows in New Orleans and also kept alligators, for which he became known locally as "Alligator Levy." He was a sign painter by trade and a frustrated artist, acquiring a very large collection of paintings. He adamantly refused to part with them, and they never provided the monetary reward that he envisioned. Herman was also an avid guitar and flute player. He and Rosa were Orthodox Jews. In addition to speaking Polish (or German) and English, they also spoke Yiddish.

Descendants of Marx Levy (1866–1930) and Gertrude Coralie Castro (1872–1905)

They married when she was 19 and he was 26.
Their children:
1. Albert Allen, B (01-11-93) D (08-20-81)
2. Edmund Hermann, B (09-15-94) D (05-31-58)
   Edmund married Louise Edna Albert, B (02-08-98) D (07-15-88)
   Their children:
   1. Edmund Conrad, B (07-27-20) D (03-18-84)
   2. Jocelyn
   3. Norman
   4. Hubert
   5. Barbara

3. Arthur Herbert
   Herbert married Aline Lopez
   Their children:
   1. Arthur Herbert, Jr.
   2. Allison Marx

4. Rudolph Levey (1899-1975) *Changed spelling*
   Rudolph married Elenoir Risher (1901–1961)
   Their child:
   1. Rudolph, Jr. "Rudy" (1921–)

5. Gertrude Coralie "Aunt Lee Lee" B (03-19-01) D (11-05-37)
   Coralie married Tilghman G. Chachere "Uncle Jack" B (04-18-94) D (08-12-61)
   Their children:
   1. Naomi, B (02-17-21)
   2. Ethel "Skippy" B (11-07-24)
   3. Tilghman G. Jr. "Buddy" B (01-20-23) D (01-16-91)
   4. Robert, B (11-28-28) D (09-20-77)
   5. Elizabeth "Betsy" B (12-17-30)
   6. Coralie "Dickie" B (07-10-35) D (04-29-64)

Descendants of Albert Allen Levy and Henrietta Catherine Schaeffer

Henrietta and Albert were married at St. Francis of Assisi Church in New Orleans on August 14, 1916.
Their children:
1. Maxine Rose, D.C., B (10-04-17) D (09-28-03)
2. Gertrude Mary, D.C., B (11-15-19)
3. Muriel Agnes, D.C., B (10-07-21)
4. Albert Allen, Jr., B (03-11-24) D (10-25-92)
5. Francis Xavier, B (06-10-25)
6. Mary Louise, B (12-01-28)
7. Joseph Anthony, B (12-29-29) D (05-27-79)
8. Michael Henry, O.M.I., B (05-08-31)
9. Louis Vincent, B (09-27-33) D (06-28-99)

The first five children were born at 1123 Royal St. in New Orleans. The last four children were born at Hotel Dieu Hospital in New Orleans.

4. Albert, Jr., and Beryl Meirer, B (11-19-23) D (02-20-52) Married (02-18-43);
Their children:
41. Albert Allen III, B (03-23-44)
42. Kathleen Theresa, B (08-14-46)
43. Arthur Louis, B (09-03-47) D (12-10-71)
44. Thomas Michael, B (10-18-48)
45. Mary Ann, B (11-07-49) D (08-05-99)

All the children were born in New Orleans, LA

4. Albert, Jr., and Effie Theodories, B (12-16-23) D (04-08-92) Married (01-11-75)

5. Francis and Marion Margaret Dueñas, B (10-16-25) D (02-12-62) Married (11-27-48);
Their children:
51. Francis Xavier, Jr. (Frank), B (11-11-49)

Vestigia

    52. Linda Rose, B (03-07-51)
    53. Stephen Victor, B (11-14-52)
    54. Gail Theresa, B (04-25-56)
    55. Daniel Alan, B (09-06-57)
    56. Ann Elizabeth, B (11-11-59)

Francis, Jr., Linda, and Stephen were born in New Orleans, LA. Gail was born in Lancaster, California. Daniel and Ann were born in Pomona, California.

5. Francis and Mary Elizabeth Naughten, B (12-21-31)
Married (09-24-69)

6. Mary and Edwin Trawick Brown III, B (09-05-26)
Married (06-14-52);
    Their children:
        61. Christopher Edwin (Chris), B (06-10-53)
        62. Beth Ann, B (01-31-55)
        63. Rebecca Ann (Becky), B (07-31-56)
        64. Brenda Ann, B (12-12-57)
        65. Bridget Ann, B (04-27-59)

All the children were born in New Orleans at Hotel Dieu Hospital. Ed was born in Biloxi, Mississippi, and he and Mary lived on the Westbank of New Orleans in Algiers.

7. Joseph and Eileen Gannon, B (08-18-27)
Married (06-30-56);
    Their children:
        71. Sharon Anne, B (03-30-57)
        72. Mark Joseph, B (04-20-59
        73. Katherine Mary, B (09-27-61)
        74. Karen Elizabeth, B (03-18-63)
        75. Maureen Theresa, B (04-17-66)

All the children were born in New Jersey, and the family home was in Manasquan, NJ.

9. Louis and Lorraine Anita Roth (12-30-30)
Married (10-10-59);
   Their children:
      91. Lisa Marie, B (08-03-60)
      92. Louis Vincent, Jr., B (12-11-61)
      93. Lance Michael, B (01-05-63)
      94. Lon Martin, B (07-28-64)
      95. Lyle Anthony, B (11-07-65)
      96. Les Daniel, B (11-10-67)
      97. Lori Ann, B (07-02-69)
      98. Lange Jude, B (12-30-72)

All the children were born in New Orleans, LA

41. Albert III and Dottie Miriam Samanie, B (08-18-50)
Married (03-24-79);
   Their child:
      411. Joseph Louis Hebert, B (03-05-74)

42 Kathleen and John Edwin Poirrier, B (02-03-45)
Married (08-31-68);
   Their children:
      421. John Ashton Poirrier, B (08-20-70)
      422. Nicole Kristin, B (10-11-74)
      423. Babette Henriette, B (04-05-80)

421. John Ashton and Lara Hartman, B (10-03-72)
Married (09-01-94);
   Their children:
      4211. Wyatt Sebaston, B (04-19-95)
      4212. Taylor Marie, B (12-16-96)
      4213. Connor Louis, B (05-20-98)
      4214. Jared Levy, B (11-10-99)
      4215. Morgan Kiley Rose, B (04-27-03)

422. Nicole and Michael Thibodeau, B (04-09-74)
Married (08-16-97)

423. Babette and Scott Landon, B (11-24-76)
Married (10-26-04)

Vestigia

51. Francis Jr. and Bonnie Bess Wood, B (01-28-45)
Married (11-24-80)

52. Linda and Gerald W. Weppner, B (05-10-50)
Married on (04-06-73);
   Their children:
      521. Vincent Michael, B (01-03-85)
      522. Gabriel Gerard, B (05-03-88)

53. Stephen and Joanne Marie Reif, B (11-25-53)
Married on (02-02-74);
   Their children:
      531. Amy Theresa, B (03-07-75)
      532. Elizabeth Marie (Beth), B (12-06-82)
      533. Pamela Mary, B (05-25-84)

531. Amy and Jeffrey Thomas, B (02-04-68)
Married (11-06-99)

54. Gail and Steve Henry Abert, B (06-19-50)
Married (03-25-78);
   Their children:
      541. Brian Christopher, B (09-25-81)
      542. Scott Anthony, B (05-14-83)
      543. Maureen Elizabeth, B (07-14-90)

55. Daniel and Cruz Nerey, B (10-17-60)
Married on (10-27-84);
   Their children:
      551. Serena Ann, B (08-28-85)
      552. Michelle Marion, B (02-18-87)
      553. Rachel Marie, B (06-12-89)
      554. Marion Margaret, B (06-06-90)

56. Ann and Barrett Burton Sturdivant, B (06-03-55)
Married on (07-01-78);
   Their children:
      561. Victor Barrett, B (12-04-87)
      562. Tavish Burton, B (12-04-87)
      563. Alan Francis, B (07-05-93)
      564. Abigail Rose, B (08-09-04)

61. Chris and Melanie Clary, B (08-12-56)
Married (01-02-82)

62. Beth and Greg Conrad, B (04-22-58)
Married (05-30-97)

63. Becky and Ken Knight, B (07-22-56)
Married (07-04-88);
    Their children:
        631. Lowell Brown Knight, B (01-17-96)
        632. Coralie Brown Knight, B (11-01-00)

64. Brenda and Greg Bahrt B (10-04-50)
Married (12-21-95);
    Their children:
        641. Dmitry Shotochin Bahrt, B (04-13-98)
        642. Azalie Mnatsakanan Bahrt, B (02-21-00)

Note: Both of these children were adopted from Russia.

71. Sharon and Alan Arellano B (04-06-57)
Married (09-25-93);
    Their children:
        711. Aaron Takoda B (05-08-95)
        712. Eliana Josephine B (08-19-96)

72. Mark and Mary Josephine Angelo (Jo) B (03-13-68)
Married (09-12-98);
    Their child:
        721. Lauren Jade B (07-27-02)

73. Katherine and Richard Janniello (Rich) B (04-05-61)
Married (11-18-95);
    Their children:
        731. Alana Katherine B (07-21-98)
        732. Maxwell Joseph (Max) B (09-19-00)

74. Karen & Daniel Abraham Rovner (Dan), B (03-09-59)
Married (02-16-91);

Vestigia

Their children:
    741. Rachel Evelyn, B (02-20-94)
    742. Zackary Joseph (Zak), B (01-07-97)

75. Maureen and Arnold Ebreo (Noli) B (12-30-60)
Married (09-03-93);
    Their children:
    751. Theresa Seton, B (01-07-02)
    752. Katherine Elizabeth, B (06-29-04)

Note: Both children were adopted from China.

91. Lisa and Enrique Vicente Kortright, B (12-20-57)
Married (12-28-91);
    Their children:
    911. Alyssa Marie, B (11-23-96)
    912. Kristen Elizabeth Gabrielle, B (03-26-99)
    913. Enrique Vicente, Jr., B (10-08-02)

92. Lou and Twyla Antoinette Williams B (01-07-75)
Married (06-08-02);
    Their child:
    921. Seth Vincent, B (03-19-05)

93. Lance and Ann Margaret Ferchaud, B (12-27-65)
Married (12-19-92);
    Their children:
    931. Lauren Therese, B (04-24-94)
    932. Lance Michael, B (12-11-96)
    933. Justin Jude, B (06-16-99)

94. Lon and Lisa Goretti Lanoix, B (05-18-72)
Married (07-27-96);
    Their children:
    941. Hannah Noel, B (02-12-90)
    942. Lon Martin, B (11-01-97)
    943. Mariah Theresa, B (01-06-00)
    944. Nena Luccia, B (06-29-02)

95. Lyle and Pam Susan Vinot, B (03-25-66)
Married (04-08-89);

Their children:
- 951. Lyle Anthony, B (07-03-91)
- 952. Ashley Danielle, B (08-26-94)
- 953. Todd Edward, B (01-13-00)
- 954. Tyler Louis, B (01-13-00)

96. Les and Jerussa Maria Aita, B (11-04-69)
Married (07-15-95);
Their children:
- 961. Les Daniel, B (02-18-99)
- 962. Emmanuel Anthony, B (11-16-01)
- 963. Elias Paul, B (12-30-04)
- 964. Gabriel Gustavo, B (12-30-04)

98. Lange and Kristen Angelle Ducote, B (08-03-74)
Married (05-22-04)

VICTOR DUEÑAS AND IRMA MAZZOLETTI DUEÑAS: Parents of Marion Dueñas Levy, the first wife of Francis X. Levy.

(Family Tree of **Margaret McGlennon** and **Charles Mazzoletti**, parents of **Irma Mazzoletti Dueñas**, who was the mother of **Marion Dueñas Levy**)

Margaret McGlennon was born on December 20, 1858, in New Orleans, LA. She died on July 16, 1921. She married Walter Tanzley, probably in New Orleans, LA. They had one child, Mable Tanzley.

Mable Tanzley married Alfred Hanneman, and they had three children: Alfred Hanemann, Cora Hanemann, and Walter Hanemann.

When Walter Tanzley died, **Margaret McGlennon** married **Charles Mazzoletti** on January 24, 1900, in New Orleans, LA. Charles Mazzoletti had previously been married to Eliza Harvey. It was when Eliza died that Charles married Margaret McGlennon, and they had only one child, **Irma Mazzoletti,** who was born on December 30, 1901, and died on March 11, 1988.

Charles Mazzoletti and Eliza Harvey had five children: Joseph, Agnes, Ermenia, Clothilda (died at 36), and Charles, Jr.

Vestigia

(Family Tree of **Jose Marcos Dueñas** and **Lily Colby Dueñas**, parents of **Victor Dueñas**, who was the father of **Marion Dueñas Levy**)

Lily Colby Dueñas was born in New Orleans, LA. She and her sister, Ida, also of New Orleans, were the only children of Charles Colby, an English seaman, and Mary Charlotte Bronson, who was from Hartford, Connecticut, or Boston, Massachusetts.

(Unknown first name) **Ultrani**, who had a sister and a brother, was passing through New Orleans when she married **Don Bernarbe Dueñas Colan Altaguerre Villenas**, the commander of a gunboat in Spain during the time of Bernardo de Galvez, a governor of Louisiana. After Spain ceded Louisiana to France, Don was relieved of his duties, and he and his wife had two children: **Jose Julien Dueñas** and Victorio V. Dueñas.

Jose Julien Dueñas and his wife (unknown) had one child, **Jose Marcos Dueñas**.

It was **Jose Marcos Dueñas** of Villa Hermosa, Mexico, who married **Lily Colby**. They had eight children: Jose Julien, Maria (New Orleans, LA), **Victor Dueñas** (Villa Hermosa, Mexico, born on January 4, 1900, and died on June 3, 1988), Amador (Villa Hermosa, Mexico, died as a baby), another Amador (Villa Hermosa, Mexico, did not marry and died at the age of 62), Felipe (Frontiera City, Mexico, died as a baby), Manuel (Frontiera City, Mexico, killed by a truck in New Orleans at the age of 14), and Angelita (Villa Hermosa, Mexico, married Jack Church in Louisiana).

Victor Dueñas married **Irma Mazzoletti** in New Orleans, LA, in January 1925. They had one child, **Marion Margaret Dueñas**, who married **Francis X. Levy** on November 27, 1948, in New Orleans, LA.

Seven years after the death of his wife, Marion, Francis married Mary Elizabeth Naughten on September 24, 1969. She was born in New York city and came West when the family moved to California in September 1943.

Mary's father, Malachy Joseph Naughten, was born in Athlone, County Roscommon, Ireland on July 14, 1894. Her mother, Mary Elizabeth Rooney, was born in Brookline, Massachusetts on July 19, 1894. They were married at Our Lady of the Assumption Church in Brookline on May 23, 1925. Malachy died in Upland California on July

5, 1987 and Mary died in Castro Valley, California on October 17, 1980. Their children were:

Malachy Joseph Jr.	B (11-27-26) D (06-21-01)
James Rooney	B (04-07-28)
John Francis "Jack"	B (09-17-29) D (06-19-88)
Mary Elizabeth	B (12-21-31)
Margaret Mary "Peggy"	B (04-25-33)
Elizabeth Ann "Betty"	B (09-05-35) D (07-11-83)

QUOD ERAT DEMONSTRANDUM